IN

JULES DIXON

To Audrey,
Thank you so much!
Garbos 4 Life

JULES DIXON
Rainbow of happily ever afters

*To my critique group—Kristin, Meredith, Sandy, Amanda, Jackie,
Nikki, I owe you so much when it comes to this story. You challenge
me and I find inspiration in **our** story, too.*
*You've kept me writing, sane and hopeful, and it's been really hard,
but hard things are usually worth it.*
Yeah… TWSS!
<3 Jules

1

KIERA

THE CAROUSEL of suitcases made a tenth trip around, but no amount of wishing would make Kiera Redfern's lime green suitcase appear.

Perfect.

She'd packed a change of clothes in her oversized purse, always preparing for the worst. And although today ranked up there in the Crappiest Day Top Ten, she was the poster child for much worse, and complaining did little good.

But sometimes whining feels great.

The day had challenged her patience. First, a cancelled flight from Des Moines to Chicago, then rerouted through Milwaukee for a flight to Burlington, Vermont. Then before boarding, the flight attendant had insisted her regulation carry-on had to go in the undercarriage for the tiny plane's flight. Either submit to the request or Kiera was staying in Milwaukee, and there was no chance in hell of that happening.

But now, she had no suitcase, no patience, and no one to complain to.

"Fantastic fucking start to a trip I didn't even want to take," she mumbled.

Turning in a circle to find someone who worked for the airline, or anyone, she caught sight of a door labeled "Ultra Airlines Customer Service." She knocked. Once. Twice. Three times.

"They only work noon to four. Peak flight hours," a janitor noted as his squeaky-wheeled mop bucket almost drowned out his voice.

"Of course."

"Put a note under the door. They'll call you tomorrow."

Sure they will.

Kiera made the request as pleasant as possible, although she imagined her sharp-angled chicken scratch would make a handwriting expert label her an unhinged serial killer. The note disappeared under the door along with hopes of her suitcase being returned to her.

The leggings and Foo Fighters sweatshirt in her handbag would accomplish her plan to hide out in her hotel room. Then Kiera would find a moment when the ten-year time capsule was unguarded and she'd steal back what she'd contributed. Nothing but the opening of that damn capsule ever baited her to come back—not that she ever thought she'd live long enough to return to her childhood home of Monroe Falls.

Kiera sighed a long breath. There were a few holes in her plan and some decisions would be made on the fly, but she'd get them figured out before the mayor revealed the capsule and contents on Sunday.

Three days left.

She stepped in front of the chin-height rental car counter and rose to her tiptoes. "Hello, I have a rental reserved."

"Name, please?" The early-twenties man karate-chopped at the keyboard with flourish. "Ms. Redfern, your car was released because you missed your rental window."

"Rental window? I prepaid."

"Our contract states if you're over thirty minutes late, we

can rent your vehicle to another customer. We've refunded charges to your credit card. Funds take about three to five days to show up. Next, please!" He waved to someone behind her.

Is he serious?

She closed her eyes and for a moment wondered if she could teleport herself back to Des Moines. Back to the security of her modest but comforting apartment. Back to her heavenly, pillow-covered bed.

Back to sanity.

Opening her eyes, she daggered her gaze into the rental rep's. "Am I supposed to sleep here until you get a car for me in the morning?"

"No sleeping in the airport. Them's the rules." The same janitor rolled along behind her, leaving her wondering if he was some sort of sadistic information ambassador for the airport.

Fun addition to this hellish mix.

The man behind the desk kept his tone an annoyingly even timbre. "Not my job to explain options, but Four-Wheels Rentals wish you the best in your journey. Next, please."

She stared at the pen in his hand. Killing someone with a pen—in these circumstances—was it justifiable homicide?

2

ZACH

WHILE LISTENING to another voicemail from his boss, Zach Lorton shifted to his right as the car rental representative motioned him to another computer.

The argumentative, petite woman moved in front of Zach, step for step.

"I rented a car. I'm getting a car." Her insistence impressed him.

The rental representative leaned closer to her. "You need to stand to the side. If—and that's a big *if*—there's a remaining rental car at the end of the day, we'll talk. Next, please!"

But the woman in front of him didn't move. "Check again."

Zach imagined the white-blonde wisps of hair peeking from beneath her blue baseball cap turned to icicles with her frigid words.

Her voice sounded familiar to him, but at this point in his sleep deprivation, he was sure he could be dreaming while awake.

"Next!" the representative called.

Zach shoved his phone in his jeans pocket, then a long yawn numbed his hearing.

She huffed. "I need to get to Monroe—"

"Falls?" The word was out of Zach's mouth before he'd thought the situation through. Apparently, being home brought back some of his old habits.

She turned, and her petite stature necessitated her to crane her neck to look up at him. She dropped her head quickly, her ball cap shielding her face. "Yes," she mumbled quietly. The woman spun back to the reservation desk, her massive purse missing Zach's privates by the width of a hair.

His phone buzzed and he checked yet another text.

"I'm not leaving until I get a car," she whispered and seemed to plaster her body to the rental desk.

Zach lifted his gaze, skimming her backside inadvertently, and chastised himself. The ungentlemanly-like behavior was worth it, even if his mother would berate him if she saw him do it. "I'm headed to Monroe Falls. I'd be glad to give you a ride."

After working a meeting-riddled twelve-hour day in NYC, then catching an hour-and-a-half-long flight, he wondered if he was sleepspeaking. Inviting a stranger to ride with him would make his mother faint. But since his only goal was to get to the Sleepy Inn and dive into a soft, comfy bed for a few zombie-like hours of sleep, he could use the company to stay awake.

Zach's phone buzzed again.

Come on, boss. I'm on vacation. You got the memo three months ago.

"No thanks, but I'll gladly take your car," she mumbled.

"Fine. You get the vehicle, and you drive me."

Zach glanced at his phone to see another text about a meeting that wasn't for another week. Meetings, emails, voicemails, and texts were the relationships in his life. But this vacation would be different. No phone. No computer.

Just relaxing. He turned the ringer off and brought his gaze back to the woman in front of him.

She turned slowly to face him, and his mouth dried quickly.

It can't be...

Although he'd detected the familiar voice, the other major details had escaped him: round teal blue eyes, dark pink lips ... and the clenched jaw. Plus, the change of hair color confused him. No longer brown. Now her hair matched the frosty disposition he recalled. Different, but he wasn't sure he liked it.

"Kiera?" he asked. *Ten years, people change.*

Her jaw tightened like a stretched rubber band. "Hello, Zachary."

Only my mother has the right to call me by my given name.

"It's Zach, but you know that."

She turned to face the counter. "I'll take Zachary Lorton's car. He can find his own way."

The rental rep glanced over her head to him. "Are you sure, Mr. Lorton?"

"Yeah, that's fine."

Her snarky attitude had an even sharper edge than he remembered. Their families had a history she apparently still held against him. He understood why, even if she was wrong. But as wound up from work as he could get, he let the little things go as much as he could now. She could have the car. He had options.

The tone of her voice brightened as the rep pounded away at the keyboard. The change reminded him of days when they weren't adversaries and they'd been friends. Maybe ... closer than that. His hands tingled with perspiration and his heart skipped, buried feelings from the past revisiting quickly.

Seeing Kiera Redfern again isn't a little thing.

Zach could call his brother in Montpelier for a ride. As far as Zach knew, Z.E. Lorton—Zayne to friends and family—the big-shot, youngest House Rep in Vermont history was in town. Zayne might come get him. Or he'd send a car, which was more likely to happen.

Zach pulled his phone out and stepped from the line. The phone immediately clicked through to his brother's voicemail.

Come on, Zayne.

He tried the number again, glancing at Kiera. Her hair wasn't the only difference. She was…

Voicemail, again? You can't even stop being worshipped for ten fucking—

"How much?" she exclaimed as the bill was slipped onto the counter.

Oh, shit.

Zach had reserved a full-size truck. Expensive. Ridiculous. But with the unpredictable fall weather, the back roads of Monroe Falls to his parents' farmhouse necessitated the four-wheel drive. At least, that was what he told himself. In reality, his ego required something making a statement of success. A personality flaw instigated and supported by his parents.

Her glare flashed to him and she lifted the sheet, waving it like the paper smelled offensively. "I guess it's yours again. I can't afford this." She backed from the counter and tossed her purse over her shoulder. As she passed him, she mumbled under her breath, "Of course, if my father still owned half of the business your dad stole from him … maybe I could."

3

KIERA

THE JAB HADN'T BEEN necessary or mature, but having Zachary Jacob Lorton in the same room brought back a history that ignited Kiera's blood like a stoked fireplace.

Encounters like this were exactly the reason she'd come in on Wednesday night, hoping to miss the rush of reunion and harvest festival attendees. Too many people she didn't want to see, Zach hitting the top of that list.

She turned away to stem the rushing emotions. That letter in the time capsule needed to be her focus, not Zach. Written when she was eighteen and while she thought her world was ending, she'd wanted to make one last statement to the people of Monroe Falls. Maybe making them remember her, for better or worse, but at least for something other than what they did remember her for.

But years later, she'd hit a snag. She couldn't remember even half of what she'd written. A few glimpses happened in dreams, but medical complications, numerous medications, what they called "chemo brain"—lingering memory loss— and possibly extreme stress had erased many details from her memory.

No matter what it said, she was sure no one needed to see the letter.

"Kiera." Zach's pleading voice tightened her shoulders as she walked away. "Kiera!" he snapped her name. She stopped moving but didn't turn around. "I'll drive you. Just wait, please."

Kiera didn't want to give in. But alternatives were nonexistent. Student loans, rent, a car payment, and other essentials most people didn't have to buy had her budget calculated down to the penny. She'd probably max out her credit card at the hotel.

She pulled out her compact and checked her reflection, adjusting her ball cap.

Keys in his hand, Zach rolled his one piece of grey luggage toward her. He'd packed light like her, or maybe he was only staying a couple days and leaving before Sunday's capsule opening. That would be welcome news, but the fewer questions the better.

Outside the small building, he pointed to the left. "The silver one." Zach stopped and opened the rear passenger cab door. "Can I put anything in the back for you?"

She lifted her massive purse and he grabbed the strap before she'd gone far, his fingers wrapping slightly over hers. Warm and soft and gentle. He definitely didn't do manual labor. Her stomach did an unexpected acrobatic move.

"You can put my jacket back there." She shoved the coat at him.

He released his hold on her hand and set his bag and her coat into the back, then slipped his coat off and placed it on top of the pile.

"Kiera, do you need help getting in?" He touched her bare arm.

Kiera stared at his hand and appreciated how her skin tingled. "No. Thanks." She climbed into the behemoth vehicle.

Their love of sarcasm and dislike of family and societal expectations bonded them in their middle school years, but in high school, their friendship had changed. The reasons, even with years of hindsight and maturity, still hung with her. "When it comes to relationships, personal or business, someone always gets hurt," her dad had said over and over, only reinforcing her pain and volcanic feelings for Zach and his family.

The driver's door opened and she jumped at the sound.

He adjusted his seatbelt. "Are you okay? You seem off."

How would he know? It'd been ten years since she'd seen or talked to him. "I'm fine."

Zach started the truck and fine-tuned the mirrors. "If you need to adjust the heat, help yourself."

She leaned over and cranked the dial. The drizzle of rain outside was typical for October, but combined with the fifty-degree temps, it chilled a person like ice on the skin. Her tank top and jeans, meant for a seventy-degree Iowa day, weren't going to cut the indecisive Vermont weather. Kiera shivered long and deep.

Wanting her coat, she reached toward the back. Without warning, Zach made the same move. They stopped, inches separating their faces. Too close. Zach seemed unfazed, but disturbing rushes of the past filtered into Kiera's body. Anger and resentment was heaved in a different but equally unsettling direction. Her heart beat faster, and her stomach plummeted like a roller coaster.

His full lips seemed plumper in the glowing, yellow light of the dashboard. Almost like two pillows, they dared her to touch, to fall into them and find out if they were as plush as they looked.

What if we just kissed? What could it hurt?

Kiera jerked away quickly, turning to the passenger window. What in the world was she thinking? She studied the trickling rivers of drizzle and attempted everything to justify the startling thoughts. Almost celibate while in school—hell, she'd barely said "hello" to a man socially in the last eight years—her life revolved around getting her degree, then completing her training as a physician assistant, and now she was in a practice, helping others in their time of need. The commitment left little room for outside activities.

Definitely tired.

Maybe horny?

Past feelings of anger just misplaced as longing for closure? Plus, her brain wasn't working right after all she'd been through today.

Whatever the reason, desire wasn't what was rushing through her body, just … something else.

"Here." He laid a fleece coat in her lap.

The scent of his cologne permeated the fabric. Soft floral traces of lotus and magnolia contrasted with his virile exterior. Zach had always been attractive, but now he'd grown into his looks, his jaw squaring off, his brow ridge now shaped into two prominent crescents, and those full and soft-looking lips.

Just get to the hotel and get some rest. It's being back here again that's making you crazy. That's all.

"You sure you're okay?" His voice dragged her from the introspective state. "I mean, I know I'm bushed, but you look almost catatonic."

"Long day, travel and all." She slipped the coat around her shoulders, comfort causing drowsiness.

Twenty minutes later, they were on the four-lane highway headed south to Monroe Falls. He cleared his throat. "Living in Chicago, right?"

"Actually, Des Moines. I'm a physician assistant."

He turned off onto the two-lane road leading to their destination.

"What are you doing now?" she asked guardedly. Did she really want to engage him?

"After graduating from UConn, I took a job at an IT consulting firm in New York City, been with them ever since."

"You travel?"

"Yeah, mostly Dallas and San Francisco. I contracted at an insurance company for a summer in Des Moines a couple of years back. Wish I'd known you lived there."

They could've been at the same restaurant or event, and she'd never have known. The information generated disappointment, feelings as intense and passionate as back in high school, and like ten years ago, she couldn't stop what she felt.

Should've called Uber, and that letter needs to be burned yesterday.

4

ZACH

THEIR CONVERSATION HAD STAYED easy and light, until Zach asked about her parents.

"They're gone," she said.

Dead?

She stared out the passenger window and he about slapped himself. *Why didn't I know this?*

He'd been living in a bubble in his West 22nd Street apartment for the last five years. Each day like the last, unless he was traveling, but those days blended together, too.

With this knowledge she seemed vulnerable, and his heart slowed with the memory of their last interaction. A high school party where words were thrown around in the heat of a moment, fueled by alcohol and enduring her relentless barrage of accusations. But now their arguments seemed trivial, at least to him. If she still held resentment over the past, he wasn't sure telling her the truth about the insurance business her father and his father had co-owned for fifteen years would change anything.

So he stayed quiet for the last half hour of the ride, listening to eighties music and occasionally catching her mouthing the words. The road was so familiar that Zach imagined he could drive it in his sleep. He'd come back for the weekend needing a break, a few days to get away from the constant bombardment of requests and demands from his clients and his boss. And getting to see his best friend Dragon perform with his band in their hometown would hopefully round out the relaxing weekend.

He turned down the Bon Jovi song and headed onto the main strip of town, only about six blocks long. "Where are you staying?"

"Sleepy Inn," she said after a long yawn.

They came in on the east side of the town. Zach had missed a turn off mostly because he was still chastising himself for making her look so despondent. He drove past the only hair salon of the small town, the Cut-Up & Dye. The owner BJ Coleman took a class in NYC to refine her skills with African American hair. She taught Zach what looked good on him and how to care for his hair. His brother's and sister's genetics took after their white father more than their black mother.

Next came the Oink, Cluck, & Moo butcher shop, and he chuckled at the sign. *Still crooked, like always. Drives Dad nuts, nothing less than perfection for him.* And then they drove by the sheriff's department. Sheriff Dogwood was probably at the community center, enjoying his nightly entertainment of Texas Hold 'Em.

Zach pulled into the Sleepy Inn's parking lot. Kiera threw open the passenger door and jumped out like she couldn't wait to get away.

An annoying drizzle of rain spat and sputtered onto Zach's bare arms. She still had his coat, but he wondered if she kept it, would she need to talk to him again? Plus, now he had hers. He grabbed her coat and his bag. His parents invited him to stay on the farm, but he'd made arrangements here. Some because their home was fifteen minutes outside town and Zach wanted to be near the action, plus, his best friend Dragon would be returning to Monroe Falls and would need a place to crash when his liquefied coping skills drowned his common sense. But if Zach was being really honest with himself, he didn't want to have to hear how fantastic his brilliant brother and amazing sister were doing. The expectations of greatness couldn't have been clearer growing up. Sure, he wasn't technically saving the world like Zoey or changing the world like Zayne, but not everyone was meant to.

Forgot to text Mom.

Sure enough, there were half a dozen texts from her and one from Zayne.

The ones from Mom zoomed quickly from inquiry on his location to hysteria that his plane had crashed. His brother's only said he was in Germany on business and to call a town car and pay to get to Monroe Falls.

What an ass.

He climbed the stairs to the bed-and-breakfast-style lodging. He paused as a voice boomed onto the porch through the screen door.

"You've got to be kidding me!"

The receptionist tried to deliver the information calmly. "I'm sorry, Kiera. Like I said, we don't have a reservation under your name. And I'm sure you know with the harvest festival, we're booked solid."

Kiera gripped her purse strap, her knuckles an icy white that almost matched her hair. "But … I called … months ago."

Her strength had always been one of her most attractive features to him, but he heard the break in her voice as her shoulders bounced with trapped sobs. Zach hated seeing her fighting her emotions again.

He cleared his throat. "I reserved a room with two queen beds. You're welcome to stay with me tonight."

She didn't turn around. "I don't think that's a good idea, Zach."

Sure, it wasn't a great idea, but it wasn't a bad idea. And maybe Kiera was right and it wasn't even a good one, but the solution was at least a workable one.

"I'm too tired to drive to my parents', but I promise, I'll be asleep in thirty seconds, and in the morning, I'll leave you the room for the rest of the weekend."

She turned and her teal eyes sparkled with a pooling of tears. "Just one night?"

"Just one night."

Kiera stepped off to the side, her head hung low, and she seemed to be submitting to the proposal.

After diverting questions from the inn owner about his siblings and what *they* were up to, because apparently he wasn't worth asking about, Zach led Kiera down the hallway. She stared stoically ahead.

The owners had made some modern improvements from the last time he'd been to the inn, but overall, it was still homey and yet, a little creepy. Intricate carvings laced the chair rail molding down the beige-painted hallway grounded with crimson carpeting. There was just enough room to walk shoulder-to-shoulder, occasionally brushing and making Zach wonder if his teenage hopes had never actually changed.

After fumbling with the lock, Zach swung the door open and flipped the light switch. One lamp the size of a flashlight flickered to illuminate the light-blue painted room. No TV. No dresser. Only two beds, one tiny nightstand, and a door that led to what he assumed was a bathroom.

Basic, and yet, intimate.

"It's not the Four Seasons, but the bed looks inviting." He cringed. "I mean, it looks inviting to sleep on, not inviting for anything else…"

What the hell was happening? His mouth filled with mental marbles and he gurgled out a few unintelligible words before deciding to shut up.

Kiera glanced around and sighed an exhausted hiss.

"Why don't you use the bathroom first?" he offered.

She shuffled to the closed door in silence.

While she was in the bathroom, Zach continued to yawn like it was an Olympic sport. He texted Dragon to check in.

ZACH: **You in town yet?**

DRAGON: **Made it in two hours ago. I'm at WJ's.**

Jack Holland's bar Wild Jack's was well known for its Saturday night special of twenty-four-ounce ribeyes and liter beer steins—anytime. Zach was positive Dragon already had a liter or more of beer in him.

When Lester K. Perrin Jr.—Dragon's real identity—was in NYC playing shows, he couch-surfed at Zach's one-bedroom apartment. The Cobalt Dragons were all over the board in song styles and eras, which usually made for problems connecting with an audience, but since lead singer Dragon was such a shameless flirt, they made the eclectic cover song list work.

ZACH: **At Sleepy Inn. Guess who's with me?**

DRAGON: **Damn, you got game, bro. Who?**

Zach's mouth turned into an arid cotton ball. If roles were reversed, he'd be thinking "hookup," like Dragon probably was. His mother would be so proud of his mouth-before-brain behavior. On the other hand, Dragon was his best friend and knew about Zach and Kiera's past. Zach could use some support.

ZACH: **Kiera Redfern**

He stared at the phone for a minute, waiting.

DRAGON: **I'll be damned. You can close with anyone. I thought she hated you and your family?**

Hate was a strong word. She'd been sick, and the truth wouldn't have helped her get better. Fears of mortality ruled her existence and untruths prolonged her bitter feelings. His parents had directed him not to make scenes or feed into her goading and to walk away. Again, expectations that his brother and sister were able to accomplish, but that one time, he couldn't.

ZACH: **We don't hate each other and this isn't what you're thinking, gutter brain. Inn lost her reservation. Just crashing here tonight. I'll stay at my parents' place for rest of the weekend.**

DRAGON: **Whatever, dude. She married?**

He hadn't even asked, but there was no ring. Not that a ring was necessary.

ZACH: **No ring. But again, this isn't like that.**

Doesn't mean I don't want it to be … but…

DRAGON: **She was always cute. Maybe I should take a chance. Activate the Dragon charm?**

Zach's jaw tightened until he had to unclench the muscles for fear of breaking teeth.

ZACH: **Over YOUR dead body. I mean that.**

DRAGON: **That's what I figured. Go for it. Would be good if your phone wasn't the only thing you've slept with in the last few months.**

Zach shook his head at the comment. Dragon wasn't judging him; he knew what judgment felt like. The story of his family's heartbreak was plastered all over the *Monroe Monitor* headlines nine years ago. Just like Kiera, Dragon still held pain inside, and Zach wondered if he could ever help either move on.

Zach removed his T-shirt and slipped out of his jeans and into pajama pants. He'd chosen the bed closest to the bathroom, but decided to move to the one near the door so Kiera could exit the bathroom and slip into her bed without an audience.

He stepped past the end of the bed when a quick-moving body crashed into his.

Oh shit…

5

KIERA

ZACH REACHED for Kiera and wrapped his arms around her. As he uprighted her, her body recognized his touch and closeness. Her sweatshirt didn't hide the fact she'd taken off her bra and parts of her were pressed firmly against his bare torso. Hard and muscular. His chest rose and fell quickly as his hand pressed into the middle of her back, his fingers tangling into the long, hairband-bound strands of her hair.

Please don't pull. Please.

"Sor-sor-sorry," he stammered the word, his past speech impediment returning, and she recalled how embarrassed he used to get.

She stared up at him. Even through the screen of her lashes, she could see his face soften.

"I'm sorry, too." The apology sounded more sincere than needed for a simple run-in.

Zach was her past wrapped up in a human who might understand her, but right now she wanted to feel more than the hollowness of being back home alone. Her hands worked their way up his bare chest, exploring the ridges, dips, and peaks, and only rested when she rounded his neck.

She licked her lips. As much as she needed to stop, she

couldn't help but tug his head toward hers. He hesitated with only a ray of light between their lips.

Finish the distance, Zach, please.

His puffy bottom lip lightly brushed against hers. "We need to talk."

The dismissal stung, but she should've expected it. Memories, good and bad, separated them.

With tense arms, she pushed back from him. "Good night, Zachary."

Whatever her head had fabricated when it came to Zach Lorton, she needed to ignore. She dashed to the bed farthest from him and climbed in, turning her back to what had happened.

The bathroom door closed and she turned off the lamp. The black consoled her with its cloaking shield, but the silence screamed she'd made another mistake.

She readjusted her hair. If she were alone, the wig would be carefully put away for the night, but this was her life. Hair was both an accessory to hide behind and possibly a veneer to make her feel … *better*? The secret would remain hers. She didn't need pity from anyone.

She rolled to her back and stared into the darkness. Childhood leukemia. Cancer was cancer, and no one remembered the specifics except for the one going through the pain. After the diagnosis came chemo and a stem cell transplant. The words still stung, like the treatments. No one had prepared her for the haunting side effects—patchy, thin hair. After wearing scarves and hats through her senior year of high school, reality set in. Her springy brown curls weren't going to come back.

Expensive, handmade wigs were a budgeted item now. Wearing one every day meant having at least two to rotate and replacing both every three to four months, spending $500 per wig, if they were on sale and she was lucky. And when she moved away for college, she'd changed the color, maybe in an effort to become someone who hadn't been the sick friend, sick daughter. In reality, the dramatic change had only been cosmetic, not helping her to be anyone but who she was.

Kiera pulled the covers tighter over her shoulder when light from the bathroom burst into the dark room.

The rustling of covers told her he'd slipped into his bed. Zach cleared his throat twice.

"Just say whatever it is, Zach. I need to get to sleep."

"I'm *really* sorry now, Kiera."

She rolled over to face him and readjusted the wig. "For almost kissing me?" She huffed, her words dripping with sarcasm. "Thanks for letting me know. Good night."

He chuckled. "Still the same Kiera." He inhaled deeply. "I missed…"

The blank ending almost crushed her chest. He missed her attitude or her? Were they intertwined? Or did he miss being in Monroe Falls?

Zach's bed creaked as he turned. In the glow of the clock on the nightstand, his gaze fixed on her face. "Kiera, I wanted the kiss to happen."

A tremble of some unfamiliar sensation rocketed from her toes to the tip of her nose.

He continued, "But with our history, I couldn't let it happen. Hell, the last time I saw you…"

She remembered that night. It'd been some of the impetus for writing the capsule letter. "I don't want to talk about that night."

"Okay. I'm sorry for getting in your way outside the bathroom, but I want you to know, I wanted to kiss you."

So many emotions tumbled in her head. Zach had been a part of her past that confused her. Why had she taken out what his father did to hers on Zach?

Words stuck in her throat like a child swallowing a penny. "I hate lots of things I said and did in the past, but most of my anger was because I was…" Her chest burned with the memories of her childhood.

"Scared?"

She nodded. The sound of her head rubbing against her pillow swished through the room. "I took a lot of my personal problems out on you. As my father always said, 'When it comes to relationships, personal or business, someone always gets hurt.'"

Zach scooted closer to the edge of his bed. With the magazine-sized nightstand in the middle, they were only inches from each other. "What if things got confused back then and I could clear them up now?"

"Confused how?" The hairs on her arms rose. If he tried to justify his father taking from hers it'd only be the stake in her heart to close it off again. She'd finally come to grips with her parents' passings, and someday she'd release her other trapped pains, but not because of a lie.

"Kiera, my father didn't kick your father out. He *bought* your father out so your parents could pay for your medical treatment."

She rolled to her back. Falsehoods only meant to cover up his father's brutal hand and to get her to forgive the Lortons. Trust was a slippery road, and they'd driven their relationship into the ditch ten years ago.

"I'm not in the mood for lies, Zach."

"It's not a lie. And I can prove it."

6

ZACH

MINUTES ROLLED by and Zach didn't dare to press the issue.

"Kiera?" he whispered. But there was no answer.

Either she was asleep or ignoring him. There was time to discuss the topic later, and hopefully—maybe—they could come to a resolution about their differences. Even if it didn't lead to more, he'd take acceptance over animosity.

The antique stained glass window shot rays of morning light in haphazard directions. The night passed with only a couple hours of sleep. Zach was used to getting by with less than a human should.

He blinked to clear the morning haze. Kiera's back was to him. His eyes narrowed in on what he couldn't comprehend. Something was different.

Very different.

He scooted to the edge of the bed and glanced at the floor. Between the two beds was a jumbled pile of light blonde hair.

A wig? He tamped down his initial reaction of curiosity as reality hit him. His gut tightened. *Is the cancer back?*

He reached down and picked up the tangle of strands. The wig was soft, but startlingly heavy. How she managed to keep it on was impressive. Should he shake the strands out?

Should he set the piece on the nightstand like clothing she'd stripped in the night? Should he place it on her bed, go to the bathroom and hope the noise woke her, and she'd put it back on? Maybe that would save both of them from questions and answers.

He shook his head at the thought. They already had enough distrust and miscommunication between them. He didn't want more. He wanted to know the truth.

Zach sat up and slipped his legs over the edge of the bed. The skin on her head looked soft, almost like creamy silk. He ran his hand over the wig, untangling the strands as the band holding the ponytail fell to the carpet. He reached down to snatch the black circle off the floor, and when he came back up, his gaze met hers.

They stared at each other for what seemed like a minute, but he imagined was only seconds.

"Good morning." His voice cracked with dryness.

She swallowed and stared at the wig, still resting on her side.

He leaned forward, elbows on his knees, the wig in one hand and the hairband in another. "I just want to know if you're okay."

Her gaze came back to meet his. "You mean with you knowing or me knowing you know?"

"No. Are you healthy or is it back?"

She sighed. "As far as I know, the leukemia isn't back, but it's a chronic disease. Right now I'm considered in partial remission."

A few times after she was diagnosed, he'd done a little internet research. Leukemia wasn't black and white, and remission was a fickle bastard.

"Are you okay with me knowing?"

She closed her eyes. "No."

So much truth in one word. Hurt. Shame. So much he wanted to make right. But could he?

He leaned closer and his heart hammered in his chest. "Kiera, you're beautiful."

Her eyes popped open. "You don't have to say that."

Zach was now close enough to feel her quickening breaths on his face. "I don't have to. I need to, and Kiera, I want to. You are, and always have been, beautiful to me."

"I can't believe you." Her eyes snapped shut, emotions sheltered inside them.

He swallowed hard as he reached to brush a slick of tears from her cheeks. "I don't know what to say to make things better. What can I do to help you believe?"

"You can't make it better, and my believing isn't yours to change."

She was right. He couldn't change what had happened when it came to her having cancer. But he could make things right from here on out.

7

KIERA

KIERA SAT up in the bed, causing Zach to sit up straight. She swung her legs over the edge, their bodies brushing.

"Please, don't tell anyone." She snatched the wig from his hand and darted into the bathroom. Either he would or wouldn't keep her secret, but she wasn't sticking around to talk about it.

Her other wig was in the missing luggage. *Noon to four,* the janitor's words ghosted to her. Her phone was in the bedroom, but she wasn't about to go out there anytime soon.

Her stomach rumbled as she waited for the shower to warm up. She hadn't eaten since yesterday afternoon in Milwaukee. Maybe after breakfast she'd drive back to—

No, she wouldn't. No car. How much she'd forgotten overnight.

She made a makeshift wig holder out of two rolls of stacked toilet paper. The strands were remarkably smooth. Maybe Zach had taken a little time to make it presentable. He'd held the lace cap rim cautiously, but no one ever expected to be holding someone's hair in their hands. He'd looked as shocked as she'd felt.

She'd never worn the hairpiece at night, probably why

she'd pulled it off, or maybe it had fallen off on its own. Breakage happened from the pressure and friction of sleep. Then she'd have to buy another one.

She lifted the clear, securing band off her head and checked for signs of skin issues: welts, bruising, blisters, and scratches. Any found problem wasn't small.

Kiera held out a hand and tested the shower water. Hot, but not scalding. Unlike Zach's fiery topaz eyes—the definition of scalding. She swore he'd almost burned her when he'd told her she was beautiful.

His insistence about an unknown truth about their fathers' business dealings saturated her brain like the steam in the shower. Her father wouldn't lie to her.

He wouldn't.

Kiera dropped her head and let the water run down her back. If only they could be on the same page, maybe they could be friends again.

Maybe more.

But Zach was trying to rewrite an old chapter of life that didn't make sense.

———

THE ROOM WAS empty when she exited the bathroom an hour later. She shoved her phone in her purse and headed down to the complimentary breakfast. She filled a plate and found a seat by the windows.

After downing a three-egg omelet plus hash browns and three pieces of toast, she stared at purple finches on the bird feeder outside the window. If only every day could be relaxing and worry-free like this, but she had things to take care of. The list started in her head. Her suitcase. The capsule. The letter. And getting the hell out of here. She pulled her phone out of her bag to check the weather, and found she'd missed calls and a text from before eight that morning.

UNKNOWN: **Tried to call three times. If this is Kiera Redfern, we have your bag. Come to the Burlington Airport to claim.**

The text sounded like a ransom note. Kiera dialed the number.

"Ultra Airlines customer service. How may I help you?"

"This is Kiera Redfern. I believe you have my bag, and I'd like it delivered—"

"Your boyfriend picked it up."

The information tightened her hand on the phone. "I don't have a *boyfriend*. Did you release my bag to a stranger?"

"One moment." The mouthpiece was muffled by a hand. "It was a Zach Lorton."

Kiera shook her head, a storm of confusion and a little relief swirled together. "Okay. Thank you."

Kiera sat back in her chair. Zach had helped her out when she needed. He'd shared his room. He'd driven two hours to collect her bag. Her heart burned in her chest. Part of the old her whispered ulterior motives, but another part screamed she'd been a fool to think badly of him.

She watched out the window as the birds squawked like the end of the world was near when a squirrel invaded their territory.

A body stepped into her view of the animals. "Good morning." Zach's voice rumbled deep, but gently. A shiver of hope zipped through her.

"Hi. Um, hey. Did you go get—"

He rolled a lime-green, soft-sided suitcase in front of her.

She craned her neck to look up at him. "Thank you."

"You're welcome. Thought you might need some time alone, and honestly, I did too." He slipped into the chair across from her and poured himself a cup of water from the carafe on the table.

"Zach, I'm not sure what's going on here." Her heart ticked a little faster.

He sipped the water slowly, his gaze directed at the chattering and squawking outside the opened window. A slow smile crossed his face when a squirrel stuffed handfuls of feed into his mouth and took out a zigzag run from the birds.

Although his silence made her uncomfortable, Kiera couldn't help but examine his profile. Zach was the handsome, masculine version of his slender and graceful mother. A delicate nose encompassed between large, round brown eyes. Model-like cheekbones. And those pillowy lips. They'd always tortured her—years ago with the words spilled offhandedly from them, but now, with what happened in her mind when she imagined them on hers.

Zach drained the rest of his glass of water and cleared his throat. The morning sun edged his irises in gold as his gaze met hers. "Kiera, I like you. Even in high school, I liked you. I'm sure I don't have to remind you that I was a shit to a lot of people. I … I have real regrets over that. But I've changed." He reached into his pocket. "I stopped by the agency. This paper will prove what I said about my dad buying the business from your dad."

She let the paper fall onto the table. Did she really need to see it? Her parents had sold their home here after she'd left. When they died, there was nothing in savings. She worked in medicine; the truth was always expensive.

"They had to, didn't they?"

Zach nodded.

Her chest hiccupped with a swell of emotion as he reached across the table and lifted her hand into his.

"And my parents told me not to tell you, so I didn't. Sometimes we do things we know are wrong, but often doing the right thing seems more cruel."

She stared at their hands. His was so warm and comforting.

He sighed and leaned in closer, closing the world in for

the two of them. "If you don't want to see what could be here between us, I understand. But I want you to know … I do."

Kiera swallowed a baseball-sized lump of fear in her throat.

Zach stared at her lips and whispered, drawing her closer to him to hear. "I wanted to kiss you again this morning. While you were in the bathroom, I thought your phone was mine, and when it lit up, I looked at the message. I left to think and decided to go to Burlington to clear my head. But my brain only dreamed about what those pouty lips would feel like under mine."

She whispered, "I don't know." But she did know. Her eyes only focused on his lips.

Zach pushed his chair back.

This was it. He'd laid himself out there, done things no man ever would be expected to do, but she didn't have the guts to cross the bridge he'd built. Her full stomach felt like a boulder was inside.

"Want to take a walk?" he asked.

Kiera's head spun, but she nodded.

He grabbed the paper and handed it to her. "If you ever want to read it."

Her parents had loved her so much they sacrificed everything so she could have a life without worry. If she couldn't see the truth back then, could she now?

8

ZACH

SHE NODDED SO SLIGHTLY, he wondered if he'd dreamed it. But then she stood, stuffed the paper in her purse, and after handing off the suitcase to the restaurant manager, Zach followed behind her.

The gardens were bursting with fall color, orange and red in some sort of starburst flowers. He didn't have to know the flower's name to appreciate its beauty.

Like the beauty in front of him. Kiera's smile bloomed as she walked along.

On the trip to Burlington, he'd focused on identifying the big things. One, he wanted to be there when Kiera needed him. Two, time hadn't diminished his concern and feelings for her. Lastly, he had control of his thoughts and he could decipher what was a small, momentary setback, and what was life changing.

Kiera could change his life forever, if she'd only let herself believe the truth about the past and trust in him now.

She was wearing the same clothes she'd worn to bed, but her hair was weaved into two long braids that brushed the crests of her breasts.

Turning to face him, she stopped in a secluded part of the property. Her voice trembled, "I'm confused, Zach."

The words' fragile timbre cut him deep. Trust took time, but they only had a weekend.

"I'll tell you anything you want to know."

"I respected my father more than anyone in the world." She wrapped her arms around herself in a protective hug. "I don't want to think he lied to me all those years. Why would he do that?"

"I think it's pretty simple." He slipped his hand behind her neck and pulled her to his chest. "Because he loved you."

"Nothing about this is simple to me. I miss them so much."

He almost couldn't believe they'd ever been as mean to each other as they had. They both had the curse of letting words flow when they shouldn't.

Their quickening breaths started to match.

She raised her head to gaze up at him. "You wanted to kiss me?"

"I've wanted to kiss you ever since you turned around and said my name in the airport."

She stepped back as if the reality pushed her in her chest. "And you think I'm … I'm…"

"Beautiful. Then, now, always."

This was their new beginning. Trust and truth for them from here on out.

Slowly, Zach dropped his head toward hers. He stopped, like last night, trusting she'd make the decision he wanted so badly. He waited.

Rising to her tiptoes, she pressed her lips to his. The contact made his body tense, but he liked the feeling of being out of control with her.

Kiera's arms circled his neck, pulling him down toward her while maintaining the contact. She was the first to take the kiss deeper. He didn't argue. There would be no arguing today.

Their tongues tangled as he slid his arms under hers and lifted her while her hands slid across his hair. She squirmed in his arms, but never broke the pressure of her lips.

He slowed the kiss to make sure she understood how much he wanted to be right here. He would earn her heart.

Then a subtle change ripped his hope away, a little tension in her body. Her eyes were wide when he opened his.

She broke the kiss and pushed from his arms. "I'm sorry, Zach. I can't."

9

KIERA

KIERA TRIED to wipe away the sensation of his lips. But there was no use. Zach had left an unforgettable mark.

The paper crinkled in her bag. The proof of her father's love was in black and white, but also glared his dishonesty. Her mother was always one to follow whatever her father said, so Kiera wasn't as mad at her as she was disappointed.

As a PA, she'd had parents plead to limit what she said to their child, especially when it came to the bad news. "A parent knows best" was repeated over and over, and sometimes she'd assented, too. Her father was a salesman at heart, spinning things in a positive direction, and always trying to protect her from harsh truths. Like her hair and other post-treatment information, he'd told her effects were temporary, not to lose hope. She couldn't fault her doctors. Sure, the reality hurt, but when it came to this, not hearing it from the man she trusted most in life hurt more.

Kiera glanced back at Zach. He ran his hand over his closely shaved head, while his back was turned. She couldn't consider the kiss a mistake. Hell, she'd closed the distance to make it happen. Kiera reached up when her wig slipped slightly from shaking her head. Just what she needed, being outed by the haze of a *Guinness Book of World Records*-level kiss.

She instinctually walked toward town. Born and raised in Monroe Falls, she hadn't forgotten the people who helped her family. The Yees had decorated the family's Christmas tree one year. To come home from the hospital to the lighted tree had given the family hope. The Hollands had donated dinners to her parents from Wild Jack's bar and restaurant. The smell of the perfectly cooked meat always made Kiera sick to her stomach, so her parents ate in their minivan. Her father would light up a fake candle to set the ambiance. The giving and forgiving theme was always there in the community.

She looked up the street to the school. They had the capsule area staked off, but no digging had started. Soon they would.

But would they forgive all, if she couldn't get to that paper?

A familiar woman getting into a Lexus SUV caught Kiera's eye. Jenna Howard, leader of the cool—and brutally mean—girls, turned as she opened her vehicle's door with a phone to her ear.

Jenna's voice carried like a yodeler in the Grand Canyon. "You're not going to believe who I just saw. No, I heard he's back, too. Can you believe it?"

Kiera's plan to go incognito had just met its death. Tiny stabs of fear trailed her spine, tickling under her wig. A memory of the letter she'd put into the capsule flashed into her consciousness. *You lied about Wes Adams stealing the…*

The memory faded away, but she didn't need to finish it to know Jenna wasn't nice.

Jenna's thick, blonde hair glowed in a burst of sun through the lightly cloudy day. "Never mind him. Do you remember that sick girl?"

Sick girl. Remembered only for three years of her life. It was like being forced into a box and never being let out again.

Kiera turned her back and made sure her wig was in its place in the antique store window's reflection. Jenna didn't need more kindling for the gossip bonfire she was starting on that call. Twenty-four hours ago Kiera would've been mortified if Zach Lorton knew she wore a wig, but now she savored that he found her beautiful with or without her hair.

But if Jenna knew…

Kiera had been brave in facing cancer; she didn't have it in her to face people with this. She remembered their heads cocking with eyes of pity, even her mother had worn that sympathetic mask once or twice. She didn't need to see their pity again.

Kiera kept walking. Memories trailed back. First, the sheriff's office. The worst thing to ever happen in Monroe Falls was a cat up a tree or a dog in someone's chicken coop. Animals caused more trouble than humans. Except for one time—the Perrin family. The headline: "Tragedy Strikes Local Family, Charges Pending." Dragon didn't need to be put into a box of judgments for something his father had done, but this town never forgot.

Kiera had left with every intention to stay away. Undergrad in Boston. PA school in Chicago. Practice in Des Moines, moving farther and farther west. Then she'd remembered the time capsule and she couldn't let a momentary lapse ruin other people's reputations. But now, plans were getting muddled in her head. She'd never move back, but Zach was making it hard to focus on what she'd come here to do, and maybe why.

Familiar faces passed, most with smiles, some with lingering eyes. No doubt the word was already out that she'd come back. Gossip like that was sure to spread like a wildfire on dry land. Questions on why it'd taken ten years would surface and her only answer would be silence.

She neared the school. Bits and pieces of another memory

brought on by hearing the band practicing on the football field.

Nan Sotheby … Mother. Dance. Food isn't the enemy.

Kiera took another look down Main Street. The bench outside the post office where she and Zach had sat during their middle school years telling each other secrets caught her eye. Secrets she hadn't told anyone else. He knew her inside and out now.

A sign pointing down Bleeker Street read "Darcy's." Nondescript. But like a beacon from one of her favorite authors, Jane Austen, she started down the street.

Kiera shuffled to a stop when the Mills' mansion, or what could be considered a mansion in the small town, came into view. Cars parked outside haphazardly but with a friendly air. Busy people fluttered in and out, holding white paper cups in brown cardboard insulators stamped with a design.

She cautiously rose up the steps. The door to Darcy's clanked with sleigh bells as she pushed it open. A few heads turned, but Kiera was lost in wonder at what was now a coffee bar, and as a sign over the wide staircase indicated there was a bookstore upstairs. Her heart leaped happily.

Zach would be gone soon, off to his parents' home. Maybe there would be a classic story she could read as she made a plan to hunker down with a good book, a bottle of wine, loaf of bread—which, from the glass-fronted display case, she realized she could get right here—and some cheese, and hide out in her room at the Sleepy Inn until she needed to make her move on the time capsule.

She sighed, staring at the menu. So many coffee choices. But she always chose black, with a hint of cream. Heck, her blood was probably ninety percent coffee from her physician assistant studies years.

"Kiera?"

A woman in full Monroe Mariners spirit wear waved from

a small bistro table in the corner. Selma Cardenas, her mother's best friend and her parents' favorite neighbor.

Selma set her book down and crossed the room, her gaze holding Kiera firmly planted. "It is you. Kiera, how have you been, sweetheart?" Selma brought her into a hug. "Loving the new hair color." She chuckled. "Do blondes really have more fun?"

Not exactly.

Kiera smiled. "Hi. Thanks." She pulled on the ends of the braids to secure the wig. "I'm doing … good."

Selma cocked her head a little. "*Cariño*, I've known you since you were a little girl. That 'good' isn't *bueno*. Money problems? Health issues? Guy"—she smirked—"or girl problems? You get your coffee, and we'll talk."

Kiera released a tension-filled laugh as the craziness of the last twenty-four hours settled in. Of all those issues, her health had always scared her the most. Sure, it would always be in the back of her mind and caution was warranted, but now that seemed the low man on the totem pole of importance. And money, it would come and go. But the last one…

"Kiera?" Selma's voice called her back. "Wow, this must be something big."

You can say that again.

"Welcome to Darcy's. What can I get you?" A previous schoolmate, Lucy Preston, leaned across the open counter. "Selma, I didn't see you come in! It's been—"

"Six days." Selma's broad smile had always been one of her best features. Well, that and legs that turned heads of men ages thirteen to a hundred and three.

"But you're one of my favorites, unlike some of our noisier and nosier guests." Lucy's eyes pointed to a table of ladies.

Long ribbons of distress sluiced through Kiera. Those women had been friends of her mother. She turned her back to the group.

Lucy stilled. "Kiera?"

Her quest to stay incognito was crumbling like the façade on the older buildings on Main Street. "Hi Lucy, black coffee, please."

Lucy talked while grabbing a coffee mug, multitasking with ease. "It's great to see you. Back for the weekend?"

Kiera kept her voice low to not attract attention. "For a couple days. This is new." Kiera motioned to the counter and coffee makers. "Congratulations."

Lucy brushed her hand through her hair. "Oh, thanks. My cousin Carter owns it. I'm helping where I can."

The explanation sounded more than a little scripted. But Kiera's attention was diverted when more elderly women joined the group of ladies, referred to lovingly—although sometimes with irritation—as the Hens. Their cackling was as loud as ever.

Kiera remembered the group meeting at the community center where she worked to help her dad when he took a second job as a janitor. Then there was a third job. And her mom had two. Kiera did what she could, but they always did more than they should. They hadn't planned on having kids but hit the jackpot in their mid-forties with a sick one.

"Here you go. If you need refills, just give a yell."

Kiera shook from her recollections. Or regrets. There was a fine line. "Thanks."

She and Selma sat away from the growing rowdiness on the other side.

"So? Spill the beans. Who or what?" Selma took a long sip of her coffee.

"Zach Lorton."

Selma leaned back, her long, grey-speckled black hair draping behind her, making Kiera the tiniest bit jealous. "What did Zach do now?"

"He kissed me." Kiera shook her head. "Actually, I kissed him."

Selma *tsk*ed. "Was it bad?"

"No!" Kiera exclaimed, a little too loudly.

"Really? That good?" Selma's long black eyelashes fluttered over her wide eyes. "Well, why're you here with me, and not wherever he is getting more hot Zach lovin'?"

Kiera rolled her eyes. "There was no hot lovin'." She swallowed a sip of blistering coffee, but warmed from the sizzling memories. "But I think there could've been."

Selma leaned in closer. "But you got scared."

Kiera nodded. *Like always.*

"Do you want there to be some hot, hot lovin', Kiera Jae Redfern?" Selma sipped her espresso.

Kiera remembered how his eyes had turned from dark brown to sparkling topaz when he lowered his head toward hers. "Maybe, but should I? There's so much history. Bad history."

"Sweetheart, I think you've just stepped over the line between love and hate. History shouldn't matter if you want to stay on the side of *amor*."

"I never hated him." Tears pooled in her eyes. "I actually cared for him when we were younger, but things went bad when I was diagnosed. And now I find out things weren't what I thought. You knew Mr. Lorton bought Dad out, didn't you?"

"It was a private business transaction, but yes, your mother told me after you went off to college. She wanted to tell you, but your father was a very proud man." Selma shook her head. "You cared about Zach back then, but what about now, Kiera? Do you, or can you, love him?"

Kiera wiped the tear dripping down her cheek. Saying the truth out loud might scare her more than walking away from him.

Selma reached for her hand, reminding Kiera of her mother. "Whatever you decide, I'm here for you. And I'd like to see you more than once every few years, too."

Kiera sighed. Her mother's funeral four years ago was the last time. "Yeah, it's been too long. Thanks, Selma. I needed this."

"Anytime, *cariño*." Selma had always called her the affectionate term meaning "sweetie," and it reminded Kiera of all the good she'd experienced in Monroe Falls.

They finished up with some small talk and snuck out the door. Coffee was like gossip catnip to the Hens, and they'd be looking for a fix soon.

After a loving hug, Selma headed off to get ready for the teachers' float in the homecoming parade. Kiera headed toward the grocery store, hoping to pick up that bottle of wine and the bread and cheese, but the smell of Wild Jack's Monster Burgers called to her. She had a couple twenty-dollar bills for emergencies in her wallet. She'd be fine to eat one meal out. Alone.

Wonder what Zach's phone number is?

10

ZACH

ZACH HAD DRIVEN TO HIS PARENTS' and checked on the farm. His mother and father hated the crowds the homecoming events, harvest festival, and reunions brought in. Although they loved bragging about Zayne and Zoey, they always chose to go to Boston for the weekend and stay in their condo on the harbor.

He jumped in the truck. His jacket lay on the seat. The one she'd worn last night.

Why had he instigated that kiss? Why couldn't he wait until they'd cleared the air and found a little perspective?

But the kiss had happened, and she had every right to walk away. But Kiera Redfern wasn't getting away this time. He was ready to fight for her now.

As much as he'd tried to keep his phone turned off, he was hoping Kiera might call him. But she probably didn't have his number.

His phone buzzed and he jumped. *Just Dragon.*

DRAGON: **Lunch at Wild Jack's?**

ZACH: **Be there in 20.**

DRAGON: **Cool**

THE INSIDE of Wild Jack's hadn't changed. Same bar. Same booths. Same—

Kiera.

She sat in a booth to the right. His nerves jumped around like a cursor on a computer screen. She was the one with decisions to make; he'd decided his path.

He forced his stutter to remain caved. "Kiera, hey."

Her eyes were wide when she met his gaze. "Zach … I didn't know you were … I mean, I… Shit." Kiera blew out a long breath. "Please, sit." She motioned a hand to the other side of the booth.

He slid in tentatively. "I want to talk."

"Yeah. Me, too." Her fingers toyed with silverware, sending small tinkling noises though the air. "I don't know where to start."

"How about with telling me how you're feeling?"

She chuckled. "Yeah, you want to hear all about that, I'm sure."

He leaned across the table and pressed his hand on hers. "I do. I promise."

Kiera's gaze met his. "Confused, yet happy. Curious, yet scared."

That was a lot to decipher and his experience with women, or lack thereof, didn't help. "Let's start with the—"

"Zachie Lorton! It's been forever." A redheaded woman with an order pad and fire engine red fingernails waved a pen at him as she stepped up to the table. Rachel Manchester, a waitress as long as Zach could remember.

Kiera rolled her eyes.

Jealous, Miss Redfern?

"Hey, Rach. How are you?" Zach asked. He could be polite at the very least. After all, he hadn't been much of that in high school.

"Been sad. You want to make me feel better?"

Kiera huffed. She never had a problem standing up to Zach, but other girls had occasionally gotten the best of her. He remembered her talking about how horrible they could be to each other. Zach threaded his fingers into Kiera's, skimming his thumb along her skin. A faint flush pinked Kiera's soft cheeks.

Rachel tapped her pen on her order pad. "Can I get you a drink? Maybe a liter of beer?"

"Just iced tea and a Monster Burger, no onion, please."

"Huh, that's exactly what *she* ordered." Rachel glared at Kiera before throwing her curly, waist length hair over her shoulder as she walked away. The woman always had been a hundred and twenty pounds of trouble.

"So, which side is better—walking toward us or walking away?" Kiera asked with a snip in her voice.

Zach faced her. "Neither, because I think I've made it clear I'm only interested in one woman." He didn't lower his voice and he didn't stutter. "Only you, Kiera."

She slipped her hand from his to adjust her hair. "Well, we've established that you can kiss."

"Thanks, and same to you. But I don't want only kissing, Kiera."

Kiera swallowed a long drink of her tea. "Do you really think we could work? We live in different states. We have jobs and friends there. We—"

"We could have each other." He was done with excuses. "Let's stop thinking up reasons to change what's here. I know you felt something in that kiss. I sure as fuck felt it." His voice quieted. "Kiera, you always had me. Even when you didn't know you had me."

Her gaze popped up. "I never—"

"Bro, I almost thought you didn't make it, but now I see you found a better date." Dragon leaned against the booth's edge, hair in the chaos only he could pull off. "Hey, Kiera. Zach said you were—"

"Can I talk to you over there?" Zach stood and pushed Dragon to move.

"Yeah, sure. Bye Kiera, hope to see you later."

Zach walked him over to the bar. "I'm gonna need a rain check."

"Wow, bros before—"

"Don't." He lowered his voice. "We're getting somewhere. She and I might actually have a chance. And if that means brushing you off for a meal, when I've had about a thousand with you in the city, then yeah, she's before you today."

Dragon's head reared back, his bloodshot eyes widening. "Whoa. I thought maybe she was just a little fun for the weekend."

A pit opened in Zach's stomach. "You didn't say that to anyone, did you?"

"Well, last night…" Dragon shoved his hands into his jeans pockets and rocked on his combat boot heels.

"What the hell, D? I let one little piece of info slip and you go telling people…" His stomach clenched. "You didn't tell anyone we were sleeping together, did you?"

"Well…"

Kiera was already struggling with letting him in. If she knew people might already think they were hooking up, she'd be right back to wondering if she could trust him.

"Who and where?"

"Mona, Kevin, and Jimmy, right in that same booth last night."

"Great. Just fucking great."

"I'll text Mona and tell her it's a secret."

"There's no secret, because we didn't have sex, Dragon. We talked and I tried to get her to open up. She finds out and—"

"I promise, I'll make sure they don't say anything."

Dragon ran a hand over his product-laden hair, calming the chaos.

"I'm holding you to this promise. No shirking. No buts."

Dragon nodded. "You guys going to the bonfire tonight?"

"Was going to ask her to go with me." Zach rubbed his palms on his jeans. "Why does she make me feel like a teenager again?"

"Don't know, but I like seeing you all messed up like this. It's pretty damn entertaining."

"Thanks, man." They did a quick bro hug, and Dragon headed out. Hopefully, he'd find Mona and the guys to set them straight, although Zach needed to talk to Mona Yee, too. He'd been prick number one to her in high school. Like Dragon, he needed to own up to his past.

The food was on the table. The juicy, use-two-hands hamburgers hit the spot. When the check was delivered, Zach quickly paid. Kiera pleaded to pay for her portion, but spending the time with her was worth more than the thirty dollars it took to satisfy the bill.

Outside Wild Jack's, Kiera yawned.

"Ride back to the Inn?" he asked.

She nodded, back to the silence of last night. It worried him, but he pushed it aside to help her into the truck's cab.

Zach climbed into the truck, warmth of the sun radiating into his back. He slipped on his sunglasses. "You okay?"

"Just still tired. Didn't sleep well last night."

He had to take a little blame for that. "Probably gave you a lot to think about?"

She cringed with a cute smirk. "Little, but you snore."

"I was wiped out. Sorry. Tonight will be better."

Her grin dropped. "Maybe we shouldn't stay in the same room."

"Oh." Zach turned into the Inn's parking lot. Maybe having him sleeping in the bed next to hers might be more than uncomfortable and she'd get even less sleep. *Can't blame her.* "I-I-I can stay at my parents." The stutter hit him when his guard was down and he was disappointed.

Kiera pinched her eyes closed. "I'm sorry I'm being so wishy-washy. This is all so sudden and…"

"Crazy?"

She opened her eyes and played with the ends of her braided hair. "A little. All that time I spent being mad at you, when really it was my dad I should've been mad at."

"Hey, your dad did it all to protect you. He was a great man and my parents had huge respect for him. Which, from first-hand knowledge, is not an easy feat to accomplish." He parked the truck.

Kiera reached for the door, but stopped with her back to him. "I just wish he would've respected me."

Zach followed her. He'd get his things and head to the farm. There was no reason to insist on staying.

Inside the room she crawled onto the bed, curling into the fetal position. Zach grabbed his bag and retrieved his toiletries.

"Please don't go."

He wondered if his head was making up the plea. Stopping at the foot of the bed, Zach waited to see if she'd repeat the request.

"Stay, please."

He set his bag down and headed to his own bed. They only had twenty minutes until the homecoming parade, but he'd gladly skip the floats, band, and advertisements from the area businesses to be with her. Plus, horses and Zach had a hate-hate relationship, so he wouldn't be missing their literal shit-show finale.

"Will you lay with me?"

He spun to her. This woman turned him in circles. Inside and out.

Climbing onto her bed, he made an effort not to disturb her. He'd let her make the first move, if any.

Within seconds, she was scooting toward him and had her head tucked under his chin and her body pressed to his. He slowly moved his arm over her waist and rubbed her back.

"You wanna take off your wig?"

"Ugh." She rolled to her back. "Yes. I saw more than a few broken strands this morning from sleeping on it."

"Can I?" Zach asked softly, wondering if he was overstepping some boundary.

"I guess." Her body rocked with a shiver as she sat up. He faced her and reached out cautiously. She leaned toward him. "Just lift at the edge and it'll slip over the gripper."

There was so much he wanted to learn about her life.

"I have a second one in the carry-on, so don't worry about ripping it." But she flinched when it caught for a second.

"How much does one of these cost?" he asked.

"Five hundred."

"Dollars?" He paused with the wig cresting the crown of her head.

"No, goats," she deadpanned, then broke into a smile. "Good ones aren't cheap."

The hair felt heavy in his hand as it slipped off her head. "How do you wear this? Isn't it—"

"Heavy, bulky, rubs, and can be annoying as hell, but not like there's an alterative. My natural hair's so thin and patchy, there isn't anything else I can do."

Zach stood. He lifted the handle on his suitcase and slowly lowered the wig onto the makeshift stand.

Back on the bed, she snuggled against him again. When he'd been a senior in high school and she'd been a junior, he wanted to tell her what his feelings really were, but Dragon would caution him. He'd been right. She wasn't in the right place back then. But maybe if he had...

He brought her closer as her body relaxed, and a long sigh took her into sleep.

SOFT LIPS PRESSED TO HIS. Warm body against him. Fingers caressed his face.

Dreams never felt this good. This real. This special. He parted his lips and his tongue met…

Kiera?

He opened his eyes to find her eyes wide and hopeful. Kiera was a dream with reality.

She raised her eyebrows slowly before backing away. "Sorry, I couldn't resist."

Zach couldn't have stopped the smile, even with a gun pointed at his head. "By all means, continue."

"The last guy—only guy I've ever been with—asked me to keep the wig on. He couldn't deal with the truth. I want you to know how happy I am to have it off."

His hands slipped gently down her face. "I only want you to be yourself and to be happy."

Her broad smile warmed his gut like nothing ever had.

"Can I touch it?" he asked.

Kiera's eyebrows crested inward. "What '*it*'?"

Zach chuckled. "Your head."

Her body immediately relaxed, but she smirked, raising her eyebrows playfully. "Oh, was kind of hoping you were talking about something else."

Now he wanted to touch her everywhere. To know her body. To know what noises she made. To find out what made her go crazy in his arms.

"Maybe I was."

Kiera held his gaze as she lifted her T-shirt over her head. *Gorgeous.*

He swallowed hard. "How are you so calm? I feel like my heart's got a ticking time bomb in it." His thumb grazed her nipple though her bra and she arched her back, pressing her breast into his hand.

She lifted his T-shirt and brushed her fingers along his abs, his muscles tightening as if to show off. "I don't know why I'm so calm. Maybe this feels right. Even if we don't end up going past this weekend, I'm pretty sure I'll never regret getting to touch … *it*." She giggled after the words.

This was the Kiera he remembered. Confident and clever and sexy. He grabbed the back of his shirt's collar and pulled it over his head.

"Holy shit. Jackpot." Her gaze swept his chest and abs. He'd filled out from his high school days.

"I still play basketball three nights a week, but work's been kicking my ass lately with sixteen- to eighteen-hour days. I've been off the court for a couple weeks."

Her brows knitted closer. "That's not good. I mean, I work twelve-hour shifts some days, but not *every* day. What do you do to release stress?"

He lowered onto her body and ran his lips along her neck. "Glad to know you care and this is a good start for relieving stress."

But for him this wasn't just sex. Their time together was more than two people meeting a base need for a moment of euphoria; it was two people strengthening a connection.

"I promised myself I wouldn't text or answer work emails or phone calls this weekend," he continued, "and so far, except for a momentary freak-out by my mother and a couple texts with Dragon, my phone's now in my bag. If I hadn't seen your text this morning, I could've gone all weekend without seeing a phone."

"Great idea. I'll do the same." She pulled her phone off the small nightstand and powered it off, throwing it onto the other bed. "Where were—"

He kissed the words from her lips. This was where they were meant to be.

11

KIERA

KIERA'S EQUILIBRIUM TWISTED. His lips pressing against hers spun her head like a ride at the Vermont State Fair. His hand rested on her hip, but as his tongue tangled with hers, he moved his hand down until he cupped her ass, encouraging her to wrap her leg around him. Through his cargo shorts, the outline of his body protruded.

She broke the kiss. "Shit, Zach. You've grown in lots of ways."

Zach chuckled, stood and pushed his shorts to the floor, then his boxer briefs.

Their relationship would never be the same. All she craved was him. Had she always wanted this? Kiera could be herself, not pretending, not hiding. The trust from long ago had never left.

His warm hands cupped the top of her bare head as he pressed his body onto hers. His warm lips explored her neck, tingles rising in places she'd never experienced. Her body rocked, tiny explosions leading to bigger ones. Zach worshipped her body with his lips, a hand slipping beneath her back to unhook her bra. His gaze met hers as he pushed up on his strong arms to watch her discard the unwanted fabric. His warm chest pressed back to hers and they both released a satisfied moan.

Kiera lifted her hips and ground her body against his, silently begging for a release. "Zach, please. I need you." She moaned every syllable.

"You ready, baby?"

She nodded. His long fingers cupped inside of her leggings and swept them down her legs.

"Fuck." His gaze trailed slowly up her body.

Commando. The one thing she'd forgotten to pack in her purse. By his raised eyebrow, he didn't seem to mind.

"Condom?" she asked.

He grabbed his bag, and in seconds dropped a foil packet next to her hip. His fingers skimmed over her body and down, until they teased into where she wanted him to be. She reached for him and slowly teased her hand up and down his hard cock.

He stilled. "God, you're so fucking beautiful."

In his shadowy eyes she saw the truth; he believed the words. Truly and honestly believed.

He fumbled with the packet, but soon he was sheathed and pressing for entrance. His gaze held hers as she wrapped her legs around his backside, and he dropped his hips to meet hers, filling her like no man would ever again.

Their bodies tangled, and he slowly built the tension to a screaming level.

She needed him in her life. There was no turning back.

Kiera let her body take over, nature and passion converging until her body shook under him. Fireworks of pleasure she'd never experienced before seared through her body, exploding in rapid succession while he drove deeper and harder, prolonging her orgasm until he met his own release.

With his breaths fast and hot, Zach pressed his face into the side of her neck as his weight became a welcome blanket.

The silence wasn't awkward like she'd imagined. She wrapped her arms around him and held him.

After pecking her lips, he pressed up, his chest muscles tightening. "Be right back." He stood and peeled the condom off.

She rolled over onto her stomach as he walked to the bathroom, his tight, bare ass glaring his perfection.

He turned. "More condoms in that bag. We're gonna use them all."

Kiera liked a prepared man. She giggled while staring at the part of him returning to a flaccid state. "I'm up for it, if you are."

"Give me five minutes and all of me will be up for anything."

Kiera rolled to her back. *A day in bed with Zach?* She'd had many days alone in bed when she was the "sick girl," but unlike those, she was looking forward to this one.

12

ZACH

THEY MADE love three more times, missing the parade and the homecoming pep rally bonfire, but nothing could've been better than having his arms wrapped around Kiera. Watching her, holding her, enjoying these moments with her, nothing prepared him for how he felt after. And the smile on his face probably had "This guy had sex!" written all over it.

She asked if they could go to the pumpkin patch, so they jumped in the truck and headed off. The local attraction held mostly good childhood memories for Zach of family outings and playing hide-and-seek in the corn maze. And one not-so-great night when his sister Zoey had been temporarily lost in the maze and Sheriff Dogwood had to call in reinforcements because, as he put it, he had "the night blindness." A lawman who was only good during daylight, apparently. Zach never understood how Dogwood was still a county sheriff, but in a small town, lots of things gave way to tradition over common sense.

"You hungry?" Zach asked Kiera after he paid the fee to get in.

"Little."

He was ravenous, like he was waking up from a coma. Maybe he was. He definitely felt more alive than he ever had.

They stopped by a food stand, and he bought a smoked turkey leg the size of a newborn baby and she chose a large bowl of clam chowder. They devoured every single morsel and drop of both.

"Hey, guys, the bonfire is still going, if you're interested," a former classmate offered, and pointed to a secluded area as he walked by.

The bonfire lit up the area a warm orange glow when they walked down the leaf-covered alley. Zach estimated the crowd to be thirty or more. Kiera grabbed for his hand. Her viselike grip squeezed the blood from his fingers.

"You okay?" he asked.

"Don't think I thought this through. Orgasms clouded my brain, I guess."

If anything, he was seeing things more clearly now, and he selfishly wanted to let everyone know they'd made up. Not how they'd made up like Dragon had insinuated. All everyone needed to know was that the past was in the past.

But if this is too much for her…

"Lorton!" Dragon's social lubricant was in full force. Beer sloshed over the edge of a cup as he shoved it at Zach. "Dude, I'm already a twelve-pack in. Catch up!"

There would be no catching up. Zach wasn't a big drinker. Kiera squeezed Zach's hand and glanced up uncertainly at him. He squeezed back, rubbing his thumb up and down hers. Her shoulders dropped and a small smile perked the taut edges of her lips.

Zach leaned down to her ear. "If you want to go—"

"Kiera!" Dragon wrapped his arms around her before Zach had a chance to intercept his drunken affection.

Zach lowered his voice. "Dragon, back off, dude. Maybe ask, before you accost someone next time."

Dragon stepped back. "Oh, she knowz hows I am. We uzed to be friends, right, K?"

Kiera backed away as Dragon's alcohol breath veiled both of them. Her gaze met Zach's, and the same concern he'd faced the last dozen years was there on her face.

She smiled. "Great to see you, Dragon."

"I'd recognize that beautiful voice anywhere."

Mona Yee always had a poker face Zach had been able to break with words—harsh and cruel words—but this time, Mona seemed to be playing the better hand. She quickly diverted her gaze. "Kiera!"

"Mona!" Kiera pulled Mona into a long hug. Their genuine enthusiasm for seeing each other lessened some of his dread. Maybe friend-by-association worked here, and Mona would forgive and forget.

Mona stepped back, but still held Kiera's hands. "Hope to get to talk to you this weekend."

"I'd like that." Kiera returned to Zach's side.

"Have a great night, K. Talk to you later." Mona's dark eyes flashed to Zach, displeasure and loathing radiating into him.

In that moment, he was transported back to high school, his parents' faces replaying that exact same look. Whereas Zayne had every teacher—and their parents—wrapped around his fingers, and Zoey excelled in school activities and raised thousands of dollars for charities, Zach was never good enough. Never smart enough. Never involved enough. Never talented enough. So many expectations he couldn't meet. They didn't want to be embarrassed by their children. Zach fucked that up. The demands for different behavior had slowed over the years, but his behavior had evolved, too. There was never a good time to admit to being a person even you hated, but if he was truly a changed man, Zach had to prove it to himself first before others would believe.

"Mona?" Zach called out. He mumbled her name again

while his brain arranged what he wanted to say. He calmed himself. "Please, can we talk?" *God, just don't let the stutter come back.*

Her dark hair sliced the air like a knife as she spun toward him. "Yeah?"

"I'm sorry for how I treated you in high school. It's one of the biggest regrets I have." He glanced down at Kiera. "One of many." Zach stepped closer to Mona and she crossed her arms. "I'm not that guy anymore. Hell, I regret *ever* being that guy. I wanted to say I'm sorry." He tried to rub some of the tension out of his neck, but it was useless. The stiffness was a little extra penance for taking his frustrations with his parents out on Mona and others.

Mona's gaze flashed to Kiera with concern. "You have something to do with this?"

Kiera shook her head. "I'm lost here. What's going on?"

"This is all me, Mona." Zach straightened his back. He desired forgiveness, but he'd take tolerance.

Mona's face softened, just slightly. "You know, Lorton, there was a time when I wanted to deck you."

"Please don't." Zach had seen her right hook played on a couple of girls. He didn't want to be looking for his teeth in the moonlight.

"We're cool." Mona's smile could disarm a Secret Service officer. "Thank you for apologizing. It really means a lot."

Zach extended his hand confidently.

Mona shook with a hard and lasting squeeze. "But if you hurt Kiera, I will put my foot so far up your ass, you'll be tasting leather."

Zach swallowed hard. *Well played, Mona.* "Understood. Thanks, Mona."

Mona waved them to follow. "Come on, everyone loves a s'more, even previously jerky fools who apparently are big teddy bears now."

Kiera snuggled into Zach's side as they walked over to the picnic table covered with food.

Could really go for s'more of this woman by my side…

13

KIERA

KIERA DOWNED a s'more at Mona's insistence. Several people had approached her, and she was quickly finding her blonde hair didn't really hide her at all. Her acceptance was necessary, but painful and ongoing. Since the past wouldn't change, she had to.

Zach nodded to his right. "I'm gonna go check on Dragon. He's hanging on to that keg faucet like it's a bomb button and if he lets go, we'll all go up."

She pulled him down by the fabric of his shirt. "Don't be gone long, okay?" Her lips brushed his.

"I'll be right back, promise."

Mona slipped in front of her. "Could you explain how you and Zach happened? I seem to remember you had some pretty … not nice things to say about him and his family not too long ago."

Kiera smiled, the feeling of warmth growing in her chest. *How* it happened wasn't quite clear, but she could recite *what* happened clearly. She relayed the mundane details, finishing with, "My room reservation at the Inn … wasn't. So he offered to share his room for the night."

Mona giggled, and the sound took Kiera back to middle

school sleepovers. "Yeah, Dragon let it slip that you two were getting it on last night."

An odd darkness crept in on Kiera. "What?"

"Dragon showed us the texts from Zach, saying you shacked up in his room. Not like it's a big deal. What you two do alone in a room is all good, right?"

"No. Not all good. We didn't have sex." *Not last night, at least.* Kiera's gaze met Zach's across the flickering flames. He smiled, but she couldn't.

That's what he wanted.

Mona's head cocked and she shifted in her boots. "Zach's message made it seem like you did—but I could've read wrong. Dragon seemed to think it was going down." She waved to some new arrivers.

Zach wasn't here with her; he was here to embarrass her. Kiera could do that well enough on her own.

Mona grasped Kiera's arm, garnering her attention. "I'm sorry if I upset you." Her sincere face reminded Kiera of every visit by a friend at the hospital or in her bedroom at home. "I'm sure I have it wrong. Maybe you should talk to him. I've got to go—check on something." Her quick excuse to leave also reminded Kiera of every visit by a friend when she was sick.

She tried to put on a brave face, like always. "We'll talk soon."

"You bet." Mona's hand patted away some of Kiera's tension, but bringing her gaze back to Zach only returned it tenfold.

Kiera crossed the area to Zach. "So I'm just some booty call you can talk about with your friends?"

"What?" Zach's jaw tightened and his eyes flashed to Dragon.

"Mona just told me you texted Dragon we were having sex last night."

Dragon jumped in. "Kahara, this's my faults. I mizsunderstood da text." Every word slurred and spittle gathered in the corner of his mouth.

She ignored Dragon. He had his fair share of problems, too.

"I can't trust you." The words hurt coming out, even if they were the right ones. "I hate that I can't. I wanted to, but I can't." She straightened her back. He wouldn't get the satisfaction of seeing her break down.

"But you can. I didn't mean—"

"To share something to embarrass me? But you did. You did, and now I'm feeling exactly like it's high school all over again!" Her voice had risen past the control level she was attempting to maintain and everyone had quieted. "You haven't changed at all."

"Hey, let's get you out of here." A warm arm wrapped around her shoulders.

She looked up and found a familiar face, Eric Cardenas, Selma's son.

"Kiera, please. Let me explain," Zach pleaded, but her legs kept her moving away from the sound of his voice. "Please."

The begging broke a fragment off her heart. She put a hand to her hair. Had he given away any of her other secrets?

Kiera could hear voices outside the truck as she climbed in, but she used her braids as an effective shield for her face.

Soon the sound of tires crunching over gravel brought her out of the daze she'd put herself into for self-protection.

"Sleepy Inn?" Eric asked.

She nodded, collecting her thoughts.

He turned his truck out of the gravel parking lot onto pavement. "You okay?" His voice was deeper now, but as timid as she remembered. Eric's chiseled jawline and dark charcoal hair had always made him look older than he was, but his eyes had a youthful glint, like his mother's.

Her hands shook in her lap. "I'll be okay." The truth was

she didn't know what she was or what she would be, but she had practice at feigning.

"I heard Zach's little speech to Mona, seemed genuine. Sorry he proved himself wrong."

"No, you're not." Her words laced with sarcasm.

Eric had admitted a crush on her long ago. They'd worked it out amicably, as Kiera always thought of him as a brother, but he'd never hidden his feelings about Zach.

Eric chuckled. "Guilty. Never liked him, and I thought you didn't, either."

"I didn't like what I thought his father had done, but turns out I was wrong. My father was the one with the secrets."

Eric shook his head. "This town eats secrets slathered in gossip for lunch."

The thought made her stomach roller coaster. A fragment of the past that was etched on a piece of paper hidden in the time capsule crept in. *Eric Cardenas ... mother ... sister?*

Eric tapped his fingers on the steering wheel with agitation. "So you forgave Zach?"

Tired of lies and dreading the real truth, she needed to at least release a little of the burgeoning boil of regrets. "I think we forgave each other, but now…"

"Do you like him?"

Even if she did, Zach had tainted her feelings with his reckless words to Dragon. "I care about him." She shook her head at the thought. "Maybe too much."

Eric turned toward the Sleepy Inn. "He's been driving behind us this whole time. I don't think this is over. Do you want me to stay?"

Her logical side, used for diagnosing medical conditions and determining treatment, kicked in. Dragon had a mouth the size of Lake Ontario. Useful for singing, not so much when it came to keeping secrets. *Idiot.* She'd deal with him later. But honestly, who was she to condemn? She had her plate full of the same.

Right now, she'd deal with Zach.

After stopping his truck along the stacked limestone wall separating the parking lot from the Inn's manicured lawns, Eric's gaze flashed to the rearview mirror. "He's waiting at the back of the truck."

"Thanks for the rescue and ride, Eric." She leaned over and kissed his cheek.

Eric chuckled when Zach rocked the truck by leaning forcefully against it and then kicking a tire. "He hurts you again and I'll be ready, probably behind Mona, to take him down a notch—or ten."

Kiera stepped from the truck. The light jacket she wore only took the chill off for seconds. The bright harvest moon splayed its glow like a flood lamp over the parking area. Kiera stood her ground as Zach approached and Eric drove off slowly. The path to the front door was only a few steps away. She could avoid him, or she could find out whatever was on the other side of this madness.

"Why, Zach?" The words steeped with hurt and weren't exactly the ones she wanted to say.

Zach sat on the thigh-high wall, the stones creaking under his weight. "Let me show you my phone. I tried to stop Dragon from assuming last night, and I asked him to talk to Mona and set her straight, but alcohol acts as his best friend." He kicked a large rock across the gravel parking lot. "Hell, alcohol's his only friend most days."

Even astronauts on the space station would be able to see Dragon's issues. She appreciated that Zach cared so much for his friend. But she wanted to know her feelings were important, too.

"That really humiliated me." She swallowed. "I'm hurting in all the places I wondered if you were meant to heal."

"I'm sorry, Kiera." Zach reached out for her, but she stepped back. "It was stupid to tell Dragon you were in the room with me. Coming home has turned me back into the stuttering, awkward, no brain-to-mouth filter guy I was, but I swear, I'm not that guy anymore." He shook his head. "I'm not."

Kiera wanted to be mad, but watching his head drop and his hands digging into his jeans pockets, she couldn't.

She was in Monroe Falls because mistakes happened. A few more memories had tingled inside her mind after seeing people at the bonfire. Although some of the people on the list of transgressions might laugh off what she'd said, there were a few who wouldn't.

"I forgive you."

His head lifted and his eyes brightened. "Thank you." A simple reply, but sincere, and what she wanted to hear. He stood and stepped close. "When you walked away, I was reliving high school all over, too. I wasn't going to let you go this time, Kiera."

She loved hearing the words and was enjoying the almost-fairytale, but in reality, they lived over a thousand miles apart. Eighteen hours driving straight through. Three-plus hours by plane.

But after facing death, she understood living held risks, too. Was she ready to take the chance of her heart being the broken part of her this time?

He hopped down and stepped close. "Wanna go inside?"

Sleep. That was what she wanted. "Yes. But no more sex until we've figured out what this is between us."

He nodded.

She tipped her head and glared. "I need to hear you say it."

"I want to figure out what this is between us, too, so until then, no sex," he said, with a little smirk, his lips tempting her to kiss the side they were raised on.

"Don't look at me like that!"

"Like what?" His big brown eyes fluttered as he feigned chastity.

Zach was everything but innocent in her eyes. Strong. Confident. Sincere. And sometimes he was wrong … and a goofball … and highly irritating. But he could be hers, and that frightened her most.

A good night's sleep would clear her head.

Only sleep, Kiera. Don't even think about it.

14

ZACH

ZACH WOKE to find the room empty. Kiera's bag still sat at the end of her bed, but she was gone.

He inhaled a long, cleansing breath. *Probably at breakfast. Chill.*

He glanced to the clock. Ten hours of sleep? *Shit.* Sleeping five hours a night—if he was lucky—caught up with him.

Zach's phone buzzed in his bag, but he was sticking to his promise. Ignore. Make better choices when it came to work and personal time. Regain himself again. There were better things to spend his time on than answering another email about the same old problem.

The door creaked open, and the smell of breakfast wafted in with the rush of air. He sat up in bed, the covers piling on his thighs.

Kiera turned to him with two covered plates stacked in her hand. "Good morning, freight train. There's coffee in the hallway. Can you get it, please?"

How do I put this?

He wasn't proud of his lack of control, but he wasn't ashamed. "Gonna need a minute, so I don't frighten children or the elderly."

Her eyes dropped to his crotch and rolled theatrically. "Men," she said with what he assumed was phony annoyance. "Fine, hold these and I'll get the tray."

He balanced the plates on his thighs. She returned carrying a small silver tray with condiments, two cups, and a carafe of what smelled like caffeine heaven.

She poured a cup and handed it over. "They get the beans from this new coffee place in town, Darcy's. Loved it when I had a cup there yesterday with Selma."

"Ms. Cardenas?" He almost moaned but stopped himself. Every guy in high school had a crush on the hot American History teacher from Colombia. The rasp of her Spanish accent held every guy's attention, and impressing the teacher was a final exam.

"Ew. I know what you're thinking, and stop. She was my mom's best friend and she's like an older sister to me."

"Sorry, but *Ms. Cardenas*." He moaned her name to razz Kiera a little.

"Stop it!" She stifled a giggle. "She's still drop-dead gorgeous, and she thinks I should go for it with you." She sipped her coffee.

"And what do you think?"

She plopped onto the end of the bed. "I think … we need to take this slow." But she leaned over the covered plates and placed a soft kiss on his lips. His heart did some kind of fancy BMX trick in his chest.

"Breakfast in bed?" He opened the top plate and found a pile of pancakes, French toast, bacon and sausage. The second plate was covered with scrambled eggs, hash browns, and a cinnamon roll. He set them off to the side and she handed him a plate. He piled on half of everything and dug in.

"Football game tonight?" he asked, after swallowing a mouthful of French toast smothered in real maple syrup.

"Sure. Maybe go to Darcy's after this? I hear they have a great collection of books."

He loved reading, and anything that made her light up like that was going to happen. "Deal."

Amicable silence carried the rest of the conversation as they devoured almost every morsel of food on the two plates in record time.

He leaned back against the wood headboard. "Probably should shower."

"Yeah." She looked away, twisting a napkin in her hands.

"I'll go first and be quick." He stacked the plates, finished his cup of coffee, and stood to move the used items to outside the door for now.

He jogged the three steps to the bathroom. Unlike some older hotels, a cloud of steam almost immediately filled the room.

While rinsing his hair and humming a mash-up of his favorite songs, the curtain glided on the metal rod and a body pressed into his back.

"I thought you might need help washing up." Kiera's voice was soft like her body.

"Be my guest."

She grabbed the washcloth and soaped up using his body wash. The fuzzy bubbles trailed down his spine and along the inside of his leg, tickling his balls into taking notice. As much as he tried to force flaccidity, his body disobeyed his pleas. The washcloth slipped lower, then around to his stomach. Mounds of softness pressed into his back and his eyes closed to enjoy the attention.

"If you turn around I can get the rest of your front." She whispered the words on a breath.

When he turned he met softened eyes and her chest lifted quickly. The washcloth slipped to the floor with a splash as she stared at his mouth.

His hands cupped her head gently as he dropped his mouth to hers. The kiss reminding him of their height differences, and that he needed to help her.

That is what I'm meant to do.

As he lifted her, she wrapped her legs around him. His cock resting between them as their bodies pressed together, blood rushing to his groin making him hard in seconds. He turned and with one hand angled the showerhead to the wall to warm the tile before resting her back against it, but never breaking the connection of their lips.

Her kiss became deeper and fiercer. Their tongues danced into each other's mouths as she quickened the pace. She moved slightly and his cock slipped to press at the entrance of her body.

She backed away and stared into his eyes. "Yes, please."

He slid into her body slowly, feeling every smooth ridge, every slick plateau, every tight millimeter of her body encasing him. When buried deep, he stopped to make sure she was still okay and the approval hadn't been a mistake.

"Do you want me to pull out and get a condom?"

"The Pill. I'm covered, promise."

You'd be a beautiful mother. It wasn't time to share that thought, but he wanted to.

He dropped his hips and slid back into what made him lose his control. This was where he was meant to be. The little things weren't important and control was overrated. She was the big thing in his life now.

The beads of water trickled down their bodies. Her hand slipped between them and she arched her back as her fingers worked her own body. Every moment captured in his mind like a cherished Polaroid.

Their breaths combined into one single existence, holding time and reality at bay. Her head fell back as she closed her eyes and allowed him to drop his head to her chest, worshiping her with his mouth.

He needed her. She was the part of him he'd known was missing, but didn't know how to get back. She writhed with every movement of his body. The past cleared out for a future he could see and hoped he could help her to see, too.

Zach thrust faster to meet her approaching peak. Legs weakening slightly, he held out. He would be her strength.

Kiera's gaze came back to his. His name brushed from her lips in reverence. "Zach." The beauty of her body pulsing around him almost made his brain crash to a stop, but his body kept on to meet her release. He thrust one last time and his body pulsed into hers. As he came down, he dropped his forehead to hers.

"Kiera Jae Redfern, I love you. I always have."

15

KIERA

THE STEAMING WATER quickly became freezing cold to her body.

Had he really said what she'd heard?

His lips pressed to hers, almost seemed to keep her from talking, but she could tell he was only sealing their time together.

"You okay?" Zach asked as he brushed droplets of water off of her eyelashes.

"I don't know."

"It's true, Kiera. I always cared for you more than friendship. And I definitely regret not telling you."

She unhooked her ankles from around his back. "I ... I don't know what to say."

"You don't have to say anything. I understand it's quick and maybe a little crazy, but I wanted you to know."

Quick? Little ... crazy?

Her brain numbed with fear. "I need to wash my hair."

He set her feet to the shower floor. "I'll go get dressed. Take all the time you need."

Her body shivered under the falling water. Kiera didn't

want to make the water warmer. She wanted to feel a chill. Maybe it would snap her out of her daze and she'd know what to do.

———

KIERA'S second wig was a little shorter than the one she'd been wearing. She curled the ends to give the strands some movement and swept the bangs into a decorative barrette. A pair of jeans and a teal Monroe Mariners T-shirt with a black sweater tossed over her shoulders fit the bill. Not remarkable, just her.

Maybe spending the day together would cement exactly what Zach meant to her. Or just confuse her more. She stepped out of the bathroom.

"Wow." His gaze floated up and down her body. "I'm a lucky guy, that's for fucking sure. You're gorgeous."

Warmth spread up her chest to her cheeks.

Darcy's was only a short walk, but Zach wanted to drive. There wasn't a reason to argue, which with their past was refreshing.

They grabbed cups of coffee at Darcy's counter. After overhearing Kiera listing off all the books she'd love to see upstairs, the barista consulted with someone, then handed Kiera and Zach a key for the first editions room. They made their way up to the bookstore and found the room labeled "Norbert's Nook" as directed by the barista. First edition books packed the walls, releasing a musty and time-aged scent.

She searched shelves, discovering books from her childhood, and remembered losing herself and her problems in those stories.

Little Women.

A Wrinkle in Time.

The Chronicles of Narnia.

Then, the one she'd read a hundred times while she was in the hospital. *Anne of Green Gables*. Hardback. Little corner fraying, as to be expected. She examined the front cover picture and every page. Not a single tear.

But … cha-ching. The cost of a hand-tied, natural-hair wig. She slipped it back onto the shelf.

"You like that one?" Zach slid in next to her, his arm wrapping around her waist. She let herself fall into his body.

"Yeah, but it's a little over my budget."

"What's your budget?"

"Thirty bucks?"

He reached for the book. "Let me get it for you."

"Zach, it's $475."

"Where's the checkout?" He didn't flinch and held the book with respect.

She grabbed his arm. "Really, it's too much."

His eyes softened at the corners. "Ten years, Kiera. Ten years I could've been showering you with attention and gifts, things you both want and deserve." He pressed his forehead to hers. "Baby, this isn't even close to enough in my mind."

"I'm just not comfortable with you spending that kind of money on a book for me."

His jaw tightened, but slackened quickly. "I understand." The book was placed on the shelf and he backed away. "If we're not going to buy something, maybe we should go take a walk to the falls?"

"I walked there this morning." She'd needed to commune with nature, a place where she'd gone to think in the past.

He slipped his hand into hers. She loved the warmth and security he offered. "Then we can go do something else. Shoot pool at Wild Jack's? Pumpkin patch again, but better this time?" Zach lifted her hand and kissed the back tenderly. His eyes sparkled. "Back to the room?"

She rose to tiptoes for a long kiss, breathless when they parted. "I want to go to the falls—with you."

They hopped in his truck.

"Back way or along the trail?" he asked.

"I took the trail this morning. Maybe start at the entrance this time?"

He chuckled. "Like common tourists?"

"Like we're civilized." She cocked her head with attitude.

The sun was in full force when they pulled into the parking lot. Guided by his grip on her waist, she slid out and ditched her sweater in the truck's cab before heading down the path.

"I saw Mr. Mills while I was walking here this morning."

Zach stopped. "The teacher who had the accident with Carter Jensen's sister?"

"Yeah. He's back."

"Almost flunked me in twelfth-grade English. My parents have their suspicions about that accident, but sometimes people here think too much."

Kiera couldn't disagree. She grabbed Zach's hand and led him down a trail to a rocky area where the mist of the falls would cool their bodies and the shade of a couple aspen trees would protect them from prying eyes.

Kiera's heart beat fast as she pointed for him to sit. She stepped between his legs and he rested his hands at her waist.

His coffee-brown eyes completed his tall, dark, and handsome look with honesty and hope.

"This is where I used to come when I couldn't deal with everything happening in my life." She sighed. "Zach, I'm afraid of what'll happen on Sunday when we both go home and a thousand-plus miles separates us."

"Kiera—"

"Please, let me finish."

He nodded and his hands slipped to her back, skimming and soothing.

She swallowed hard, the weight of the moment settling in. "But … if you're willing to make the effort, I'll do the same."

"I've waited over ten years to hear that. And it sounded better than I'd ever imagined." His youthful happiness took her back to high school, in a good way.

"Now, I'm still paying off college loans—big college loans —and my credit cards are maxed out, but I'll buckle down. And when I have weekends off, I'll come see you. When you have weekends off, you do the same, and we'll see where we can go."

"I know the wait and sacrifice will be worth it. I promise it will. "

"You're worth everything to me, Zach."

His hands drew her closer, his head resting under her chin. "I used to think I wasn't worth anything."

"What?"

"Well, at least worth less than my brother and sister."

"Less what?"

His arms wrapped her tight like he didn't want her to get away. "Less of a person, less of a man. Just a lot less in general."

She held his head to her chest and he snuggled in tight. "Why?"

"My parents. Their expectations. My failures. The list used to haunt my dreams."

She closed her eyes. Kiera had heard a couple of his parents' comparative speeches in middle school. There were stark disparities between Zach and his twin Zayne that had little to do with skin shading or hair color. Zach excelled at basketball, but his parents saw that accomplishment of low importance when grades, respect, and family participation in the community came first. They weren't bad people; they just didn't understand their children weren't meant to be what they wanted. Their children were meant to be themselves.

"I never knew." She didn't know what more to say.

"It got so bad that I considered…"

Kiera's breath hitched and tingles of thankfulness crawled her body. *I would've missed you.*

He shook his head, as if to erase the statement that made her eyes burn with salty tears. "But I didn't, because they would've seen it as a blemish on them, and even as much as I hated the way they were, I couldn't do that to them. So I became a jerk for most of high school to make others feel my hatred for myself."

"Zach, you don't have to be anyone but you. People liked you, including me. I remember you stood up for yourself like I wished I had. I don't know what to say about your parents, they are who they are. But how do you feel now?"

"Some days, I feel like Zayne had it easier than me, but because I've worked harder for what I have, maybe I appreciate it more. Like you. Although I wish we could've been together ten years ago, I don't think I'd be the same guy. I'm not okay with how things went in my past, but I'm definitely happy to be part of your life again." His gaze met hers.

"I woke up this morning thinking I was dreaming."

His hands cupped her face, drawing her forehead to his. "This is no dream. I love you, Kiera."

Her stomach dropped while he seared her memory with a slow, soft kiss.

She swallowed fear to feel. "I … I don't know what to say. I care about you, Zach, but…"

A flash of black handwriting passed quickly. *I never had the guts…*

He smiled. "You don't have to say anything."

The falls created a symphony to drown her pitching thoughts. She turned in his arms, and they sat there, holding each other, the moment as warm and soothing as the sun on their faces.

Zach … and love. Had they always belonged together?

She'd once thought people were going to lose her. But now when she was the one who had someone to lose, she froze, unable to say the words that effervesced inside her, like the mist brushing their faces. Was this her chance for happiness?

Chances. She had to take at least one today.

16

ZACH

THE FOOTBALL GAME was tied up before halftime. The Monroe Falls Mariners fought hard, but the opponent's defense had everyone on their feet.

Zach wrapped his arms around Kiera and she leaned back against him. The ease of their connection made him wonder if long distance would be enough.

"Zach, bro."

Zach straightened at the familiar voice and looked to his right. "Zayne? I thought you were in Germany?"

"Got in last night." Zayne's gaze tracked across Zach's chest to Kiera. "Who do we have here?"

Zach pulled her closer, but Kiera wasn't tense.

"Hello, Zayne. Nice to see you again."

"Kiera Redfern?" Zayne chuckled. "This is unexpected. Nice to see you, too. Mom and Dad know about this?" He lowered his voice, directing his question at Zach, but Zach ignored him.

Motioning for his brother to move so they could slide out of the bleachers, Zach's gaze searched for his brother's fiancée. "Where's Charlie?" She wasn't fond of small towns, but Zayne would ply her with Coach bags and Tiffany jewelry to make an appearance.

"Back in Montpelier. She had a birthday party to go to. I texted you, but now I know why you didn't respond."

Zach had stood up to his own challenge. No phone. And knowing Zayne was coming to Monroe Falls would've only made him want to leave it back at the hotel, anyway.

"Is there an after-party tonight?" Zayne asked, waving at an older couple. "Excuse me, I have to go check on one of my favorite donors." The politician in him was always on.

Kiera stepped beside Zach. "Want to leave?"

"Let's finish the game, then maybe we'll bounce."

"I'm gonna go use the bathroom."

"Want me to walk with you?"

"Nah, I think I can remember how to get there." She pecked his cheek, but he couldn't help himself. His lips brushed hers and a long shiver trailed through her body.

"You cold?" he asked, running his hands up and down her sweater-covered arms.

"Little."

He slipped off his jacket. She swam in it, but the vision reminded him of high-school letter jackets and wishing she'd wear his. "You're amazing," the words slipped from his mouth effortlessly.

She stilled, the roar of the crowd rising as the team scored, but she never pulled her gaze from his. "You're amazing, too, Zach. Inside and out."

Kiera filled the spot that made him feel less.

"I'll be right back." Kiera walked away.

Zayne stepped beside him, phone to his ear. "Yeah, yeah, Zach's here. Not sure. Maybe his phone's dead." He covered the speaker. "Corbin's calling me 'cause he needs to talk to you."

The fact his brother had become close friends with his

boss didn't bother Zach. But the fact Corbin was using the connection to get ahold of him while he was on vacation did.

Zayne held out the phone. "He says it's important."

Zach shook his head. "Everything's important to him." *Everything but my sanity.*

"Sometimes we have to work hard to get what we want. He pays you well for being good at what you do, right? Be a fucking man." Zayne shoved the phone into Zach's chest.

I am a goddamn man.

Zach grabbed the phone and trailed to behind the bleachers, away from prying ears and the volume of the crowd. "Hi, Corbin."

"Zach, man, the Peterson program crashed and we can't get it back up. We need you to fly to San Fran and fix it, like yesterday. The clients are threatening to go to Tri-Syndex. We can't have that."

"I'm on vacation. You know that."

"And I also know I pay you very well to do what I ask, when I ask. This is your project."

"And I told you that program was a heaping pile of shit when we took it over last month. I was clear it would take at least six months to get it stable. This isn't news; it's the truth. They're on life support, Corbin, and they're expecting miracles you keep promising them. But I'm not God, and neither are you, so this conversation is over. I'm staying here, and I'll see you on Tuesday."

"Just need you to hop on a plane and tell them that."

"I have. They don't listen, and neither do you."

Corbin had used and abused Zach for four years. A dozen headhunters had pursued Zach in the last year with higher paying jobs. But this weekend had made it clear—there were more important things than money. Indentured servitude wasn't going to happen anymore. It was time to stand up to the tyrant.

He cleared his throat, confidence holding strong. "Corbin, I quit."

"What the fuck, Zach?" Corbin's voice transformed to his slick, salesperson shtick. "Hey, hey, let's slow this down. No one needs to quit. If you could make it back first thing in the morning, I'm sure we can hold them off until then."

"I'm not coming back. Have Wanda box up my office and send it to my apartment. I'm done with being your go-to guy who can't get a moment to unwind and take a break."

"If it's more money you want—"

"No, it's not more money. I want my life back. I want to be with the woman I love. And I want a job that allows me to do both of those. And yes, Corbin, without me, you're fucked. Best of luck to you. Goodbye." Hitting that big, red "End" button was the easiest thing he'd ever done. When the screen lit up, he sent Corbin straight to voicemail, again and again.

Zayne walked up with a barely legal redhead hanging on his arm, giggling like she'd huffed helium. "You gonna head back to NYC tonight?" he asked.

"Nope. I quit."

"Why the hell would you do that?"

Zach shoved the phone back at Zayne's chest and let it drop to the ground when his brother didn't grab for it. "Because I decided to be the bigger man I've always thought you were, even trying to be like you because Mom and Dad worship you. But Zayne, I'm done trying to be you. I'm just going to be me. Goodnight."

17

KIERA

WITH ZAYNE KEEPING ZACH BUSY, Kiera figured she had about fifteen minutes before he'd start to wonder where she was.

She took off on a jog the two blocks to the school.

As they'd driven by, she'd seen the hole was dug and yellow tape tied around four poles anchoring the edges. She hadn't been there for the time capsule's burial, cooped up in her bedroom with only her books. Before the stem cell transplant she'd had visitors, people who told her their secrets and fears. She'd also overheard things said in confidence when they thought the "sick girl" was asleep. Kiera had heard it all. She just couldn't remember it all.

She rounded the corner and of course, the hole had to be lit up like a manger scene at Christmas. Her heart jumped in her chest.

"Caution," the tape mocked her.

She peered over the edge. Only about three feet down, but it was a little muddy from the previous rain. She unwrapped the tape from a temporary stake. What would Sheriff Dogwood do if he caught her? Was this illegal or immoral? *Does it matter?*

She slipped off Zach's jacket and slid down into the hole, her canvas shoes sinking as they hit the bottom. Her fingers kneaded the soil. How much farther down would she have to dig?

A car's headlights flashed as it turned onto Main Street. Kiera ducked, brushing her jeans in multiple places against the muddy walls. She'd been gone for minutes now. Her hands caked with mud and sweat beaded on her brow as she dug furiously. Then the sound of metal scraping under a fingernail stopped her.

Could she really do this? Was the paper filled with only cold recollections, or were there gems of happiness? She doubted the latter. But more important, why had she written it?

She plopped back and her butt came to rest on the soft, damp ground.

The hand of mortality had clutched her. When faced with death, she unloaded the knowledge that weighed on her, heavy or light. A final farewell message to remember her for more than being that girl who wasn't there the last two years of school. But it wasn't fair to all those people. Friends and foes who were unsuspecting their truths would be known to all of Monroe Falls. Even if the reveals weren't a magnitude of death and destruction, they were still private.

She spread her legs and started digging feverishly between them again, pulling at the edge of the box. *Please don't be locked.*

Demonstrating the trust of a small town, the lid popped open and moonlight bounced off the donated items of ten years ago. A well-loved CD. A worn number 33 Monroe Mariners football jersey. A heart-shaped necklace engraved with letters she couldn't quite make out. Each of them something good and wholesome. Then at the bottom, beneath probably thirty items, there was a folded yellow paper.

Giving bad news on the color of happiness. Ironic.

Voices coming from the direction of the football field grew louder.

Is the game over, or is it halftime?

She closed the box, swiping her foot over the top and covering what she could before hoisting herself out of the hole.

After grabbing Zach's jacket, she hid behind a large pine tree and dusted off what dirt she could on her denim. Hopefully in the moonlight, the stains would look like shadows. Voices of excited fans surrounded her. She shoved the piece of paper into a coat pocket and headed back to the football field.

She thought she'd feel relief, but keeping secrets from Zach felt as bad as what she'd probably written on that piece of paper. Her feet shuffled faster with her ratcheting anxiety.

Sliding in next to Zach at the concessions stand, Kiera wrapped her arm around him, hoping he'd take away some of the unease surging her body.

"Whoa. Hey, you okay? Been gone a while." His arms tugged her closer.

Even Zach couldn't soothe the wave of nausea tumbling through her stomach. "I'm okay."

HER BODY SHIVERED EVEN though she had his jacket on.

"You sure?" he asked.

"Actually, I'm not feeling good. Can we go back to the Inn?"

"Of course." He turned to Dragon, clasping his shoulder to get his attention off the halftime homecoming coronation. "Hey, we're gonna head back to the Inn. We'll see you tomorrow night at the dinner and dance."

"Sounds good. Whoa, what's wrong with her?"

"Probably tired from traveling." Zach pulled her closer. "And Dragon, take a break from drinking tonight?"

He huffed. "My momma didn't raise no quitter." He cringed after saying the phrase. Death didn't erase love, only the loved one's existence. His father had created a bullet hole in Dragon, too. One he tried to fill with vodka on a good night, tequila or bourbon on a bad one. And by the smell of his breath, this night was headed toward epically bad.

"Dragon..." Zach grumbled with a shake of his head.

He held up his hands in surrender. "Fine, Mr. Drinking Police, I'll take the night off. Have to get ready for my big hometown debut tomorrow night, anyway. The guys are coming in and we need to set up."

Dragon wasn't fooling him. Zach brought his friend in for a quick bro-hug and swiped Dragon's car keys from his jacket. When the keys magically appeared, Dragon never questioned how or why.

"Hey, love you, man." Zach turned to walk away.

"Are you hitting on me?" Dragon called out.

"You wish." Zach grabbed for Kiera's hand, but it felt cold and like something was coating it. "Kiera, is there something on your hand?"

"Little mud. I slipped."

Zach shook off an uneasy feeling, but Kiera's silence in the truck and the way she clung to him returned his concerns.

What's going on, Kiera?

"HEY, SLEEPYHEAD, GOOD MORNING." He brushed his hand over her face, head, and down her neck.

Zach had never felt so invigorated as after ending the call with Corbin. He couldn't wait to tell Kiera about his plans. Find a new consulting job where he could live anywhere. Move to Des Moines to be with her. Marry her, however and wherever she wanted. Have children with her, if she wanted them. Maybe a dog, maybe a cat, maybe an SUV. He wanted the whole sappy story.

"Can you go get me some 7-Up?"

Sick on vacation wasn't what he'd imagined for them today, but he'd do whatever she asked to help her through.

At the 2 Pump, he gassed up the truck while her requested drink waited in the front seat.

"Zach Lorton." His name was said with disdain, reminiscent of how Mona had said it.

He turned and Eric Cardenas, the man who'd taken Kiera

back to the Sleepy Inn from the pumpkin patch, stood right next to him. Another person he'd treated poorly in high school. He should've known that owning up to his past wasn't a one-shot-and-done thing.

"Eric. What's going on?"

"How's Kiera?"

In previous years, another man asking about the woman he was dating was grounds for a broken nose or at least some hurled slights, but Kiera was his. He was sure.

Zach smiled and shook the gas-dispensing handle to get all the gas out. "She's not feeling well today."

Eric's eyes narrowed. "Like *how* not well?"

His blood pressure ticked a little higher, but Zach made effort to stay visibly unaffected. "I'm thinking a traveling bug. You know, airplanes. I swear we pay to get sick when we purchase a ticket."

"As long as it's nothing else."

Zach's past wasn't quite as "past" as he thought. *Maybe in a small town it never is.* He leaned over the edge of the truck bed. "I love her, Eric, and I'll never do anything to hurt her."

"Just words, and yours don't mean much to me. I remember the night you said the ones that made her become a different person, Zach."

His senior year and a party at Dragon's house when both their parents were away for a weekend was easily, but regretfully remembered. Kiera had showed up, even though her parents didn't know, and after taking her stinging jabs for hours, and consuming plenty of the free dumb-speech elixir provided by Dragon, Zach let go of arguments and declarations that weren't true. Words and claims he didn't just regret, he loathed himself for. She wasn't needy. She wasn't revolting. She wasn't obnoxious. He'd lashed out, unable to tell her the truth of how he really felt. How scared he really was. Responsibility for a portion of her misery fell directly on his shoulders.

"I gotta go." He needed to run a quick errand and get back to her. "And Eric, I'm sorry for being a dick to you in the locker room. You don't have a small—"

"I measure up to any guy, Zach. In lots of ways."

"I'll take your word for it."

Eric shook his head. "Take care of her, or I'll take care of you."

Zach nodded. There was nothing left to say; his actions needed to speak for him.

When he returned to the hotel, the shower was running. He knocked on the door, then turned the knob and stuck his head inside. "I've got your soda, babe."

"Thanks. Just leave it on the counter."

"Are you feeling better?"

"A little."

"Wanna go to the dinner dance?" He leaned against the doorway.

"Give me about an hour to get ready."

He thought about leaving, but she was a captive audience. "Kiera, we need to talk." Except for the splatter of falling water, there was silence.

She pulled back the curtain, adjusting it to cover her body. "Okay..." She shivered, even though clouds of steam rolled from the shower.

"Are you sure you're okay?"

"Just a little traveler's thing."

"Then maybe we should stay in."

"No, I want to see Mona again, and you promised Dragon we'd be at the band's performance. I'd really like to hear them." Her face brightened, but he could see past the façade. Something was bothering her. Maybe it was him.

"Kiera, I'm sorry for those horrible things I said to you at Dragon's party."

She sighed and leaned against the edge of the shower. "Zach, I badgered you. I made you out to be the person who was wrong, when really, my father made *me* the person who was wrong."

"You need to forgive him, Kiera. He did everything he thought was right. He was scared, too."

Kiera stilled. "He was scared?"

The decisions her father had to make, the sacrifices—he'd always impressed Zach's father. But parents weren't always right. Zach understood this better than anyone. They hid things. They said things. They could mess up.

Zach took the two steps to reach her. "Who wouldn't be? I was scared, too."

"You were?"

Emotions gathered in his throat. "Kiera, I would've been crushed if you were gone, and I'll thank God every day that we have a second chance."

"I've been scared for half of my life, Zach. I don't want to be scared anymore."

He clasped her face in his hands. "You don't have to be scared. I'm here. I'll take care of you."

"But you're going back to New York, I'm going back to—"

"I'm not going back. I quit my job last night."

She shook her head. "I don't want you to do this for me."

"I didn't. I did it for me, and for us. I'm looking for a job in Des Moines. All the hurt, the lies, and fear are now behind us, baby."

She gripped the edge of the curtain tighter.

"Kiera? What's wrong?"

"I don't know how not to be scared."

"I'll show you." He stepped into the shower, fully clothed, and held her.

The water washed the past away.

19

KIERA

SHE DIDN'T KNOW how he'd done it, but he had. Now that the letter was out of the capsule and Zach was by her side and apparently would be in Des Moines, too, there was little else to worry about. Her stomach calmed, shoulders softened.

"You have a gorgeous smile."

She didn't even realize she was smiling.

The community building filled quickly with people. The local ladies' group had outdone themselves with the decorations. Small white and deep-orange pumpkins—no doubt from the Yees' pumpkin patch—were surrounded by no-flame, tealight candles, over a burlap table runner, each piece the perfect fall touch.

The food rivaled any four-star restaurant she'd eaten in. The traditional dishes of the area were the best. The beef brisket was Kiera's favorite. The sauce was rich and herb-laden, reminding her of a dish her mother would've made. Selma brought *arroz con leche*, Colombian rice pudding. Kiera went back for seconds and danced her plate back across the room, all the time knowing Zach's gaze never left her.

Dragon stopped by their table. His eyes were lined with black, his T-shirt strategically ripped to show off what was underneath. Or maybe he didn't give a shit. "You guys hear the capsule was broken into last night?"

Zach put his fork down. "Why would someone do that?"

Dragon ran his hands through his styling-product drenched strands and gave himself a messy style change-up. "They think something was taken. They're looking for a list of things that were put into the box."

Kiera's stomach bottomed out. "Do they know who placed items into the box?"

"Nah, just the stuff in it."

The temperature had risen into the mid-seventies during the day, so the side door to the hall was open to allow for ventilation. She shivered as a burst of air circled in on her.

Zach's gaze scanned the ground behind her chair. "I thought you brought a sweater?"

"I did." She glanced around, too. "I must have left it in the truck." She started to stand, but he stopped her.

"I'll get it."

She wanted to argue, but too many thoughts fought for space in her head.

Zach stood. "D, you guys starting soon?"

"On my way to sound check."

"Just stay here and enjoy." Zach kissed Kiera's cheek as he passed by, whispering in her ear, "Hey, there's Ms. Cardenas." He flicked his eyebrows and made a moaning noise again.

Kiera shook her head at him.

Selma and Zach passed with simple greetings. "I guess things worked out?" Selma asked as Kiera pulled out a folding metal chair next to her.

Although she couldn't be totally sure at this moment, Kiera had hope. "I … I think I'm in love, Selma."

Selma's hands lifted hers and she squeezed them. "Beautiful girl, you deserve to be happy."

"I know you sacrificed family and personal time while I

was sick to make sure I graduated. I've never said how much I appreciated it, but I did … do. Thank you."

"Sweetie, you were worth every late night and every drive to Boston."

Zach returned with her sweater and his fleece jacket. *The jacket. The letter.* The evidence had found its way back to her.

Kiera gulped her wine. The alcohol burned and she coughed into her napkin.

While Dragon did a series of sound checks into his microphone, Selma continued talking about the staffing changes happening at the school. She'd retired last year, but many people weren't happy with the way the administration was.

Zach handed her the sweater, but Kiera set it in her lap. Selma's voice became only white noise as Zach slung his jacket over the back of his chair on the other side of the table.

Selma squeezed her arm. "Kiera, *cariño*, you look pale. Are you okay?"

She rubbed her forehead. "A little bug from traveling."

The band struck up and Dragon's voice boomed through the hall. "Ladies and gentlemen, welcome back to Monroe Falls. We are Cobalt Dragons and we take requests. And FYI—bribes *will* get your song moved to the top of the list." The crowd chuckled. "I'm serious. This isn't a paying gig, and I need gas money." They laughed louder, but Kiera could only manage a tight-lipped smile.

Zach added in a shrill whistle when Cobalt Dragons started up the first song. His band played, and Dragon bellowed "Best of You" like Dave Grohl and the Foo Fighters were right there in the room.

"I'm gonna get another beer." Zach leaned across the table to allow his voice to reach her over the pounding music. "You want another glass of wine?"

Kiera shook her head.

His eyes narrowed questioningly, but he diverted his gaze to her right. "Selma—I mean, Ms. Cardenas—anything?"

"Call me Selma. I'll take a glass of red wine, please."

Kiera's gaze flashed to his jacket. There was no place else to hide the paper. Her purse was back at the Inn.

The crowd clapped an enthusiastic response as the song ended.

Dragon chuckled at the accolades. "Thanks, folks. We'll be right back with our first set, need to adjust a couple things."

Kiera stood and reached for Zach's jacket.

"While they're fixing whatever, I have a little something to share." The shrill voice made Kiera's back straighten as she faced the stage. *Jenna Howard?*

Jenna waved yellow papers in the air. The colorful lights on stage spun like a kaleidoscope until everything turned dark and blurry at the edges of Kiera's vision. Her brain searched for the words on that paper, but meds she was taking when she wrote it, the chemo effects, or time itself had erased the information.

"Apparently, someone was keeping tabs on everyone back in the day. So I'd like to reveal a few of the juicy details about some people like everyone always gossips about me. Like, did everyone know that Kevin Yee took Milly Belton—Milly, there you are. Well, Milly, he took you to senior prom on a dare, then he actually found you sweet and liked you, but because the guys would have given him so much shit, he told you he didn't like you. Nice job, Kev."

Across the room, Kevin's head reared back in surprise. The room quieted to funeral level.

"Eric Cardenas—whoa, this one involves Ms. Cardenas, too."

No. No! The words shouted in Kiera's head, but nothing would come out.

"So Ms. Cardenas is not Eric's mother. Eric, meet … your sister."

Selma's eyes widened, but she didn't look at Kiera, her

stare firmly planted on the man she'd called "son" for twenty-eight years.

Eric crossed the room. "Mom?"

"Not here. Outside, please, Eric."

Kiera's legs weakened and she used a hand on the table to hold herself up.

Jenna shook the papers as if it were an official reading of legal announcement. "Let's get through a few of these, shall we? Jared Lott, you took the SATs for other people for a hundred dollars a pop because you liked taking the test. What a nerd!" She rolled her eyes. "And Louise Coleman, you let Ricky Swanson use your mom's Fairmont and he was the one who put it into the pond. And—"

"That's enough." Dragon reached for the paper.

"No, I'm going to read every single one of these. It's time the truth came out about everyone who's ever judged me. Nan? Nan Sotheby? Crap, not here. That's no fun. Well, well, lookie here. There's one about you, Dragon. Seems you let Mrs. Bleeker's chickens out of their enclosure after she called your family 'white trash.' Doc Jones's dog killed them. Apparently, killing runs in the family."

Dragon's jaw locked tight and he reached across her, but Jenna's long, red-painted nails dug into the paper. She pointed across the room. "Even the great Sheriff Dogwood gets time to shine. Anyone else know he hides cards under the table at poker games? Double standards strike again in this small town."

Dragon tried to chase her down, but she slipped through his arms. "Can I get some help? Zach!"

She scooted to the side, her voice still booming even without the microphone. "Oh … this is a good one."

"No! You've done enough." Dragon grabbed the paper.

"I know who wrote it." Jenna's gaze met Kiera's. "Never thought the sick girl had it in her."

Kiera turned toward the door, and Zach was right there, his face showing both confusion and shock.

Kiera's body felt like it was floating away. She had to keep it together. "I'm sorry."

She ran from the room, bodies blocking her at every turn and all eyes spotlighting her. Her heels clacked like lightning on the wood floor as Jenna continued her thundering recitation of the horrible words on the paper.

Kiera threw open the front door. She kicked off her heels, grabbed them, and darted across the road, behind Wild Jack's to the river walk.

It didn't matter how it'd happened.

But Jenna Howard?

She rolled her gaze to the sky and held up her hands. "You had to kick me when everything was going so well, didn't you?"

Kiera only had herself to blame. Not a deity. Not Jenna. Not Zach. Not Dragon. Not anyone on that paper.

Just me.

ZACH WATCHED Kiera scurry away and his confusion grew.

Selma returned to the room and took the glass of wine from his shaking hand. "She was angry at the world. That wasn't the real her, Zach."

"Are you okay?" he asked her.

Selma downed half of her glass of wine. Zach thought about doing the same to his beer. "I'll be okay. How about you?"

Zach swallowed a lump in his throat. The room was hushed tones of people discussing what had happened and accosting Dragon for the paper as he ushered Jenna off the stage.

Selma cleared her throat. "Kiera cared, Zach. That paper is only a moment in time. Thankfully, she's alive and she came back to us. To you."

A post-mortem gossip column? It seemed ludicrous. In the scheme of life, Kiera wasn't reporting murders or violent acts of crime, but the truth could be hurtful and some very private.

"Zach?" Dragon stepped in front of him. His voice was serious and restrained.

"Yeah?"

"You need to read this paper."

Zach couldn't imagine he needed to read anything on that paper. He was sure his reveal wasn't flattering. "I'll pass. I'm gonna go." He didn't know where. Just not here.

Dragon shoved Zach's jacket at him. "You two have something that not a lot of people get. Don't let one stupid moment ruin that. You'll regret it."

Zach beelined to the front door, ignoring questions and speculative eyes.

Even with knowing Kiera had written those horrible reports on people, he instinctually scanned the outdoors for her. He couldn't stop loving her. It wasn't possible. But he needed answers and time to think.

The papers fluttered in the coat pocket and he grabbed them before they floated off for someone else to use them in a public display of ridicule.

Inside his truck, he stared at the pages fisted in his hand. What more could they have to say that he needed to know? But if Dragon thought he needed to know, then… *Shit.*

He was nearing the bottom of the page. Her disarming nature caused people to tell her secrets. Zach had shared one of his at the falls the day before, too. But she'd exposed these people. And now she had a secret of her own—the wig—and she knew how it'd feel if someone outed her.

He brushed some dirt covering a few words.

The dirt on her hands. This was taken from the capsule.

Lines later, he still hadn't hit anything about himself. *Dragon needs glasses.*

One about Mona, one about Nan, and Dragon…

And there it was.

The words made his chest burn.

Like a NASCAR racer, he skidded the truck into a spot at the Sleepy Inn. He tore past the front desk and down the hall to their room.

Only darkness met him inside.

Her bags were still there, but where was she?

Sitting on his bed, a lump hidden in the covers reminded him of the commitment he was ready to make. He drew the carefully wrapped package out, but hid it again when he heard voices in the hallway.

Kiera?

The footsteps kept going.

He pulled his phone out of his bag and plugged it in. The five minutes for it to charge seemed like an hour. She'd written down her number for him and he used the time to look for the slip of paper.

ZACH: **Where are you? We need to talk.**

The sound of a phone buzzing in her purse on top of her suitcase made him still. She'd held up her end of the no-phones agreement.

His phone was a constant barrage of emails, voicemails, and texts. He skimmed through without reading half of them. Corbin needed to find his testicles. His amount of begging was bizarre for a grown man. And the headhunters had started their pitches of, "Heard you're a free agent…" and "Love to talk to you about an opportunity…"

The only opportunity he wanted was to see Kiera and talk to her.

She couldn't have gone far. He reviewed the places they'd been. The secrets they'd shared.

He knew where she was.

21

KIERA

THE MOONLIGHT GUIDED Kiera to her place at the falls, the same place she and Zach had sat yesterday, holding each other and allowing the silence to bond them. The soft sounds of water splashing and the roar of a river crashing from fifty feet in the air drowned a little piece of the burning in her heart and the aching in her head. There was no excuse for what she'd done.

Rustling in the tall grass made her still.

"Kiera?"

"Zach?" Her heart clopped at Kentucky Derby speed.

"Where are you?"

"Follow my voice." But her voice trembled.

In a few seconds, his shadow cast down upon her. "Are you okay?"

She couldn't look at him. "I've been better, but considering how others probably feel now, yes, I'm okay."

Zach squatted in front of her, his face shining in the moon's glow. He rubbed his hands together. "Should've worn my jacket…"

Her head dropped. "The letter was in that jacket."

"Explain to me, Kiera. I wanna understand. Why and how and ... why?"

"Everything on that letter was written while I was at my lowest. I was pumped full of meds that gave me mood swings and brain fog. They couldn't find a stem cell donor, so I was basically a walking dead girl. I thought I wasn't going to get my original life back and I hated what life I was living so, I decided to leave my mark and maybe a part of me wanted to make others feel as bad as I did. I think you might understand that?"

He nodded.

She swallowed a lump in her throat. "I thought I was going to die. Everything on that paper was meant to hurt the way I was hurting. I never thought I'd be here to watch the capsule opening and whoever was would deal. But there's no good excuse. There's no valid argument for writing things like that. I take responsibility for it."

"Did you mean everything in the letter?"

"It was all the truth, if that's what you mean."

"You're sure?"

The palms of her hands started to sweat. What had she said in that damn letter? "I ... I don't know. That's why I was sick last night. Just the thought of taking it and the thought of what was on it. I couldn't look. Those words were like reliving a time in my life that I hated."

Zach stood and stared at the glass-like water. "Then let me remind you of what you said."

She held her breath.

Zach turned to face her. "'I loved Zach Lorton from the moment I saw him in middle school and I never had the guts to tell him. Now I'm gone and it's too late, but I want you to know, I loved you.'"

The world spun with leaves, moonlight, wind, water, all a twirling mélange of sound and color. Memories buried like that capsule were raised to the surface and her heart sang.

Zach smiled. "And you just said everything in that letter was the truth."

"It was. And it is." She stood and submitted to a magnetic pull she'd ignored for years, allowing illness and lies to keep her from knowing love.

She lifted his hand in hers. There was only one more thing to say. She wouldn't worry anymore.

"I love you, Zach Lorton. Always have."

"I love you, Kiera Redfern."

His lips caressed away all her worries. Like the water fell over the rocks, the past crashed down, too, creating a lot of noise and a big splash, but in the end, everything washed downstream. The clatter was forgotten in the glassy reflection of the calm waters.

She was the falls. He was the calm river.

22

KIERA

"WE NEED TO GO, KIERA."

She'd dragged her feet for the last hour, but Zach seemed to understand why, even if he was getting a little impatient now. He rubbed his eyes. A lack of sleep probably wasn't helping. They'd cemented their love for each other for a large portion of the night, both with talking about the future and making love.

Did the door open last night?

"Did you go out during the night?" she asked.

"To make sure the truck was locked." The vehicle was a rental, after all.

Okay, just woman up and get this over with.

She stared out the room's window. Last night, holding each other, everything seemed idyllic in their little cocoon, and they'd planned to go to this morning's pancake feed, a traditional hangover remedy and a final chance for people to say their goodbyes. Kiera might be saying goodbye for good, depending on people's reactions.

"I don't know if I can do it." She packed the last of her toiletries.

He wrapped her up in his arms for the third time in the

hour. "You can. I promise, whatever you're imagining is ten times worse than what will happen. Plus, we need to get to the capsule reveal." He checked his phone and cleared the messages like swiping a chalkboard. She was impressed with his resolve to be more present and less reliant on technology. Dropping his lips to her temple, he pulled her closer. "It starts in five minutes."

They'd discussed this, too. She needed to face up to what she'd done. She grabbed her purse, then opened the door and stepped out of the safety of the room. With Zach holding her hand, she realized protection wasn't a place. It was being with him.

They had to park farther from the school than she'd expected. Her letter had probably increased interest, with people wondering what else was in the capsule.

Hand in hand, they walked toward the growing crowd. Kiera imagined whispers around them, and she pulled the brim on her ball cap down to shield her eyes from any glares. If she were approached, she wouldn't run or make excuses.

"Zach! Kiera!" Dragon called from across the street, holding a to-go holder filled with large coffees. "Coffee?"

"Thanks." She lifted one and sipped the black sunshine. "Dragon, I'm—"

"All good."

"I want to—"

"Not necessary." He held up a hand. "Someone else might want your apology, but I'm just glad to see you're still here and on the arm of this guy. You guys make me believe happily ever after can happen in more than a song."

Zach gave Dragon a bro-hug and Kiera saw him drop keys into Dragon's coat pocket. He leaned down to her. "I'll tell you later."

"Ladies and gentlemen, I present the ten-year time capsule." Mayor Duncan held up the metal box. "We'll be setting the contents along the wall over there." He pointed to a shaded area on the east side of the school lined with tables. "You're welcome to collect your item after the noon hour."

They allowed the majority of the crowd to pass through the line. Eyes lingered on her.

Eric and Selma approached, space between them, but the fact they were together gave her hope. Kiera grabbed for Zach's hand, and he held on firmly. "Selma, Eric, I'm so sorry. There's no good excuse for what I did."

Eric's gaze stayed away from hers, but Selma stepped close. She sighed. "Kiera, what you told was not yours to tell, it was mine." Kiera tightened her hold on Zach's hand. "But I understand why you did it, and since I could find neither the guts or backbone to do it, I should be thankful and, *cariño*, I am."

Kiera released Zach's hand and threw her arms around Selma. "I'm sorry. You mean so much to me. Thank you for understanding." She stepped back.

Selma brushed away Kiera's tears with her fingertips. "No crying. What was in that letter was the truth, and now Eric and I can move forward without lies."

Kiera knew what lies did to a person. She turned to Eric. "I'm sorry, Eric."

Eric's jaw was still tight. "I'm not sure I can be as forgiving as my mo—*sister* is. I thought you were my friend. You could've come to me. I'm sure you have secrets, too."

"I am your friend, and you're right, I do have secrets of my own. And not that it makes up for it, but..." Kiera lifted off her ball cap and then her wig. More attendees than only Eric stared with wide eyes, with whispers becoming full-on pointing and droning. "Bald as an eagle up there."

Eric's eyes softened, but his jaw stayed tight. "Are you sick again?"

Kiera turned to the crowd. "Everyone, can I have your attention?"

Faint hushes brushed through the crowd, and normally cheerful people wore visible scowls.

Her hand shook, holding the wig. "First, I am sorry for the letter last night. That letter was written when I thought I was going to die years ago, but I'm not currently sick. Yes, I was sick, and yes, I could be sick in the future, but as of right now, I'm okay." She rambled a little, nerves fighting to take her down.

"What you *did* isn't okay!" a voice shouted out from the crowd.

She cringed, but held her head up. "You're right. That letter wasn't okay. It wasn't even close to okay. I'm very sorry to anyone who was outed by what was written as my last ode to being the 'sick girl.'"

As she looked over the crowd a few people still had hard jaws and piercing eyes, but mostly she saw soft smiles. As much as she regretted what she'd done, she realized forgiveness started with herself. They could hate her. They could hold this against her. But she needed to stop beating herself up, loathing her past, and not let her illness define her future.

Only a few stragglers remained as Zach urged her toward the line.

The two tables were littered with memories. She examined the treasures with a new appreciation. They were nearing the end when her gaze fixed on the edge of a brown rectangle, wrapped in protective plastic.

Zach enveloped his arms around her. "That's yours."

She set the wig and hat on the table and lifted the book, the protective plastic crinkling.

Anne of Green Gables.

Kiera pursed her lips, emotions bubbling under the surface. "How'd you get this into the capsule?"

He chuckled. "You think you're the only one who can scale into a hole in the ground?" Zach leaned down to her ear.

"Turns out Dogwood definitely has night blindness. Man can't see ten feet in front of his face at night."

She laughed and kissed his cheek. "It's too much, Zach." She ran her fingers over the slightly faded profile of a woman with curled hair, pulled into a decorative pin at the back of her head.

"Babe, it's not enough. I'll spend the next sixty years of our life proving you deserve so much more, if you'll let me."

Her heart skipped. "Are you proposing?"

Dragon choked on his coffee as he walked by. "Are you?"

"Kiera Jae Redfern, if you say 'yes,' then yes, I am. If you need more time, then I'll wait until you're ready."

She'd loved him for fifteen years. Maybe a few of those, or more, were spent in denial and most squandered on worry and fear, but no more.

"I love you. I want to spend the rest of my life with you, too. Yes."

He lifted her feet off the ground and kissed her until the world spun in her head.

No more secrets or lies. Finally, she was in the place she needed to be, in his arms.

Read all the Secrets and Truths of Monroe Falls after the new Epilogue!

EPILOGUE

ZACH

"YOU LOOK GOOD IN A TUX," Dragon said while he stared at himself in the mirror, adjusting the three strands of hair that had fallen from grace.

Zach shook his head. "Amazing your head fit through that door."

Dragon chuckled. "I was talking to *you*, brother."

Today was the day. Kiera would be Zach's wife and nothing could stop it.

The room lit up as lightning cracked on a nearby pond. *Except maybe that.* Rain hadn't been in the forecast, but stormy weather didn't need an invitation to make an appearance.

Kiera had asked for an outdoor wedding. In June. Apparently, one of the hottest times in Omaha, Nebraska. But they were here. Their friends and family were here. And this was happening.

Zach smiled, so many changes had happened in such a short period of time. Their lives had taken them farther west than either had ever thought of living. Omaha, Nebraska wasn't small but wasn't big. It was diverse and welcoming, and most importantly, anywhere that made Kiera happy was where he would always go. Plus, he'd found a great job that paid for the SUV (but not a minivan, something Kiera had eye-rolled at), a big, rambunctious dog, a pretentious cat, a couple of crazy chickens, and maybe in the future, a few little feet would patter across the wood floor of their mid-century bungalow. But most importantly, he had balance. He could take days off to landscape the back yard and mornings off to fix the bathroom toilet that ran like a ghost had flushed. And days off to just sit on the back porch and watch the sun set. It was a refreshing change.

A familiar face poked around the edge of the door. "Everyone ready?" Mona asked.

Dragon grabbed Zach's shoulder. "Weather be damned. You're getting married today, Zachariah."

Zach shook his head. That wasn't his name, but arguing wasn't happening. This wedding was. "Let's do it."

Mona cracked a smile and opened the door fully. "You look good, Zach … and you look okay, Dragon."

As he passed, Dragon kissed her cheek. "Some days I wonder if I should've made a move to have you by my side."

Mona raised a hand and playfully pinched Dragon's cheek. "Sorry, but Jimmy earned my heart long ago, just like Zach earned Kiera's. We just didn't know it."

Zach's stomach rode a surf wave, almost towing him under. It was true. His heart had always known.

Kiera waited behind the door down the hallway in the Bridal Suite. He'd made sure to never see her wedding gown; the surprise would be worth it, he was sure of that. Kiera was worth everything. He was positive about that.

He stepped out and only a few drops of rain tickled the air with tiny pings on a few shallow puddles. The warm day cooled and for mid-June, it really wasn't bad. Or as bad as it could be. *Miracles happen.*

In a few feet, Zach took his place under the white gazebo trailing with a vining purple flower that Kiera had commented was one of her favorites. *Wisteria.* He'd written it down to buy one and plant in honor of their first anniversary next spring. She was right. It was a gorgeous and perfumed surround to what would be a memory imprinted forever on his mind.

The flower garden at the Gerald Ford Birthplace was one of Kiera's favorite places to go and sit. Zach figured it was her new "falls" spot. There were very few actual waterfalls in the area, so she'd taken to enjoying the element of nature readily available. And since this was only a ten-minute walk from their house, they frequented the flower-filled location almost every evening. It was the right place to get married to the right woman.

The string quartet played "Hallelujah" by Leonard Cohen. Within seconds a voice sang out. Goosebumps raced along Zach's body. *Dragon?* Dragon's voice flowed in flawless harmony with the quartet. He'd told Zach he had a few surprises in store.

Kiera appeared at the end of the aisle, a satin dress hugging her svelte body in all the right places and Zach's father on her arm to guide him to her. His gaze never left her. She deserved to be the only one taking his attention.

She stopped at the quartet and tapped a kiss on Dragon's cheek. Dragon hadn't sobered up for the occasion, but he'd made effort to stay more coherent. Zach really wondered if there would be a rock bottom and how low would that point would finally be. He'd never abandon his friend, but soon a tough love conversation would have to happen.

Kiera turned back to the aisle. Twenty people sat on each side of that runway of beauty. All their closest friends and family would watch them become husband and wife and then follow them to the Old Market area for a dinner planned by Mona. The woman was a beast at organization and as Kiera's maid-of-honor, she hadn't left one detail unpolished. Mona stepped up to Kiera and took her bouquet of white roses. A soft coral-orange ribbon wrapped the stems, a gesture of honor to leukemia survivors and those who hadn't made it.

Zach couldn't imagine what he'd do without Kiera, so their lives were dedicated to raising money for research and more effective treatments. His parents had started a foundation in Kiera's name with her blessing and to Zach's surprise. Mr. and Mrs. Lorton had done a lot of soul searching in the last few months, with Zoe and Zayne leading a campaign for them to see what they'd all done to Zach, and with a heartfelt talk they'd apologized for the past and promised to focus on making the future better for everyone. Zach forgave them, because that was what was right. Kiera made him a better person. The person he wanted to be was far from perfect, but he tried daily to find a way to reach the perfection she saw in him.

Zach's father smiled at Kiera. His glossy eyes surprised Zach. "Kiera, welcome to the family. We love you like a daughter. You make me proud, Zach. Take care of her. She's special. Love you."

"I know, Dad. Love you, too." He hugged his father and then stepped back to guide Kiera into place at the altar.

Dragon returned to the front and faced Kiera and Zach. "Welcome, friends and family." His online ordination to perform weddings had happened after a drunken night of celebration in NYC before Zach left for Omaha. Completed as part joke, part sincerity, after Kiera found out, she insisted that Dragon do the ceremony and Zach didn't argue. Who better to perform than the performer?

"Over twenty years ago, these two amazing people met. Ten years ago they hated—"

Zach cleared his throat loudly.

"Okay, they didn't really hate each other, they actually loved each other but in a *very* weird way."

"Moving on, Dragon," Mona whispered, but the crowd caught it and chuckled.

"Zach, my brother, this woman will bring out the best in you. Listen to her. Ask her how you can make her life better because I guarantee it will make yours better, too. Find ways to create a world for just the two of you. Keep close your secrets and even closer her heart. She deserves you and you deserve her." Dragon cleared his throat, as did many of the guests.

Dragon continued, "Kiera, whatever you're doing, keep doing it because I've never seen this man as truly happy, and I've seen him be miserable, so I know the difference. If there's one piece of advice I can give you, it's to take care of yourself. Sometimes in relationships we're so focused on the other person that we forget to invest in ourselves. Give to yourself as much as you give to Zach and I can't imagine how wonderful you two will live out your lives. Now, for the vows … Kiera—"

"Can I go first?" Zach asked. This was the moment when they'd lay out their deepest feelings for each other and reveal their plans for their future. He couldn't wait.

Kiera's lips widened into a broad smile. "Of course."

Zach released a deep breath. There was too much to say, but he'd have sixty plus years to say the ones he'd forgotten. "Kiera, for fifteen years my heart dreamed of having you by my side as my partner, my love, my life. Now that we're in this moment, I can't imagine there's anything more I need than you. You have a way of making me feel like I'm the king of my own life." Zach paused and collected himself. This was harder than he'd thought. *Just say it…*

Zach lifted her hands to his lips and pressed lightly, watching a small, happy shiver quake her body. "You take my darkest days and lead me to your light. You find good in me when I sometimes can't. You smile and my world becomes the best place to be. And you never cease to surprise me with your forgiving heart and thoughtful ways. I strive to be the person you are. I love you, Kiera Jae Redfern. Today. Tomorrow. And always."

Kiera raised her hand and brushed it down his cheek, collecting the trickling trail of his feelings. Her glossy gaze stayed connected to his. "I love you, too. All you need to know is that I will forever be by your side, in sickness and in health, in good times and bad, whatever comes our way, we will face it together." She pursed her lips, before sharing a smile that could melt the Polar ice caps. "And the next step of our lives will start in about seven months."

The crowd gasped and Mona dabbed at her eyes while wearing a soft smile. Zach's confusion guided along with a gently whispered, "Congrats, daddy."

The news finally slammed into Zach's brain. He inhaled sharply. "You're pregnant?"

Kiera nodded, a giggle slipping past those pouty lips he loved so much. They'd been trying, but many doctors had warned her past treatments could make conception so much harder. *Miracles do happen.*

Zach lifted her off the ground and into his arms, pulling her into his body. He whispered in her ear, "You kept a secret from me?"

They'd agreed no more secrets. They knew what those did to a person.

"You like surprises. Now kiss me, Mr. Lorton."

But he was willing to forgive her for this secret. So he did as she asked. Dragon pronounced them partners in love and life while they cemented their love to loud cheers.

As they walked the aisle, Dragon strummed a guitar and sang another song Zach had never heard before, but he'd never forget.

This Love is Forever
There were mornings when my heart called for you.
There were days when my soul wished for you.
There were nights when my mind dreamed of you.

And here you are.
Here you are.
Here…we…are.
My love is true. My love is you. My love is forever.
My love is true. My love is you. My love is forever.
Now in the mornings my heart calls you mine.
Now all the days my soul cares for you.
And now the nights I make love to you.
This is a dream.
This is my dream.
This…is our…dream.
Our love is true. My eternal love. This love is forever.
Our love is true. My eternal love. This love is forever.
Forever.
*Forever.**

In his arms was the only place she'd forever be.

~THE END~
Or is it?

Find out what happens to Dragon in the next Monroe Falls Romance coming Fall of 2018.

This Love Is Forever by Lester K. Perrin/Julia Harney Stamps

Keep reading for the Monroe Falls Truths and Secrets…

MONROE FALLS TRUTHS AND SECRETS

Kevin Yee-

You took Milly Belton to senior prom on a dare, then actually found her sweet and liked her, but because the guys would've given you so much shit, you told her that you didn't like her.

Jimmy Costello-

You cut perfect roses off of Mrs. Yee's prize winning plants and gave them to your mother for Mother's Day when you couldn't afford to buy them. Mrs. Yee saw you, but she didn't say anything cause she thinks of you as her son, too.

Dragon (Lester K. Perrin, Jr.)-

You let Mrs. Bleeker's chickens out of their enclosure after she called your family "white trash". Doc Jones's dog killed all of them. I understand why you did it; Mrs. Bleeker should apologize, so should you.

Eric Cardenas-

Selma isn't your mother. She's your sister. Your mother lives in Colombia.

Poochie Thibodeau-

Your father lives in Grantville, Illinois with a wife and two kids. Your mother knows.

Louise Coleman-

You let Ricky Swanson use your mom's Fairmont and he was the one who put it into the pond.

Mona Yee-

Made laxative brownies for the principal after he suspended you for fighting. He crapped a storm for a week, literally and figuratively.

Smitty Jeffries-

You hit on Ms. Cardenas every day, it was gross. Have some self-respect, grow up, and if you're married, respect your wife or husband.

Jenna Howard-

You lied about Wes Adams stealing the statue off the Oink, Cluck & Moo. He had to work weekends for Davis at the butcher shop to pay off something that he didn't do.

Tony Bradford-

How's that rash clearing up?

Nan Sotheby-

Your mother's vicarious dreams of dancing weren't yours. She was too harsh on you. I hope you got help for the eating disorder and you're safe now.

Lucy Preston-

Thank you for "borrowing" books from the library for me,

then sneaking them though the dog door. You made my days brighter.

Sheriff Dogwood-

Hides extra cards under the table at the poker games. Good luck poker players!

Carter Jensen-

Thank you for always sharing those fish with Dad. Some days it was the only meal my father ate and I think you kept him alive.

Carly Crawford-

Your dog, Mr. Scruffles, used to sneak through our dog door and come lay with me, but your own father ran over your dog, not my father. We were in Boston. I miss him, too.

Robin Zindel-

I saw you crying the day you tricked Mona into spraying herself with ammonia. You could've stood up to Jenna. Be you, not her.

Rick Reynolds-

You knocked Jimmy Costello off the stage risers and blamed it on Eric Cardenas.

Brett Collins-

Stop trying to be the bully Zach Lorton was. You're better than that. He was too.

Lizzie Reynolds-

Please don't end up like your mother. You're beautiful the way you are.

Liam Richardson-

You stole the statue off the Oink, Cluck, Moo. It's buried in the horse's hay barn at the Holland's property.

Bethany Olson-

I saw you kissing Zach Lorton behind the bleachers while you were dating Brett Collins.

Jared Lott-

You took the SAT's for other students at $100 a pop. You were quite successful at getting the exact score the student wanted.

Zach Lorton-

I never understood why you treated people so horribly. That wasn't the real you. I knew you.

And now me...

Kiera Redfern-

I loved Zach Lorton from the moment I saw him in middle school and I never had the guts to tell him. Now I'm gone and it's too late, but I want you to know, I loved you.

THE MONROE FALLS ROMANCE
NOVELLAS

Read all of The Monroe Falls Romance Novellas:

All stories were originally part of the Falling: Small Town Love Anthology. Several stories have added content and all new epilogues. Find out what's happened to many of the characters you came to love after their original adventures in Monroe Falls.

Between the Lines by Kristin Lee

Local journalist Emily Elliott dreams of a bigger life than the small town headlines she writes about, but she's terrified to leave behind her father as he recovers from a recent heart attack. The best part of Monroe Falls is her best friend Jared, her mainstay, her confidante. But answering a phone call meant for him leaves her blindsided when she discovers he has an incredible opportunity in front of him, one he can't pass up. Will she take a chance and follow her heart, or be left behind?

When Jared Lott is offered a dream job to write for a top newspaper in Boston, everyone in Monroe Falls expects him to take it. But the memory of a New Year's Eve kiss with Emily has him rethinking his dream. He must decide if he'll lay it all on the line by admitting his feelings or let her go with just a goodbye.

In His Arms by Jules Dixon
2018 RITA® Finalist from the Romance Writers of America®

Ten years ago Kiera Redfern left Monroe Falls and moved farther and farther away. An invitation to the opening of a time capsule triggers the vague memory of her contribution and prompts her return. No one needs to see that letter, and definitely not Zach Lorton. When heated memories become fresh temptation, Kiera has to decide between changing the past or fighting for her future.

Zach never thought she'd be there, but after a night of revelations and a kiss that can't be ignored, he's ready to help Kiera heal from the past. When his boss demands his return to NYC, Zach has a choice to make—continue the abuse that's followed him through his childhood or stand up for himself and be the man he wants to be for Kiera.

Both will find out... is it better to be forgiven or forgotten?

The Road to Us by Cynthia Morton

After calling off her seven-year engagement, Louise Coleman has taken up residence on her mother's couch, struggling to start over as a self-employed interior designer. A run-in with the handsome town grocer has her sketching designs for a new future. But when too many important decisions become unavoidable, Louise must choose between the life she thinks she wants or the future she deserves.

In Monroe Falls, Brian Mason found a chance to honor the memory of his parents, but he never expected to find love. With the chance of deportation back to Canada looming, Mason has to decide to mend ties with his only brother to stay in the country or abandon the business he's worked so hard to create and leave his new found love behind.

Take My Hand by Nikki Hyson

Secret bestselling author and hometown barista, Lucy Preston is stunned when ten years after he left, the man who ran away with her heart walks into her café. She's always hidden her true feelings, but one look at Arthur is enough to crack the walls she's spent years building. When Arthur crumbles emotionally, will Lucy be strong enough to tell him everything written in the past?

Ten years ago, a momentary distraction cost Arthur Mills everything. Determined to make amends, he's spent his time away alternating between volunteer groups until a forced hiatus sends him back home to Monroe Falls. But his childhood home is now a coffee shop, and the student he admired is now a woman whose smile warms his battered heart. Will Arthur accept lessons of love from Lucy and find you can come home after all?

Secret of Us by Wynter S.K.

Mona swore she'd never go back to Monroe Falls. But when her parents' business goes into crisis, there's no other option. She brings with her not only the uncertainty of facing the bullies that ruined high school, but also a huge secret that threatens to shred the bond she shares with her brother.

Leaving NYC for sleepy Monroe Falls is no problem for Jimmy—Kevin, his best friend, is home from war. A lifelong friendship means no secrets, but will it survive when Kevin discovers the girl Jimmy fell in love with while he was deployed was Kevin's little sister?

Hooked on You by Jacqueline Winters

Sky Emerson proved she's worthy of making partner in her sister Elaine's wedding planning business. Until…one well-known, handsy groom steals an unsolicited kiss in front of the cameras. It not only crushes Sky's dream but forces her into hiding. When Sky realizes she doesn't have a way to pay for the last available room in the small, welcoming town, she devises a harmless lie to buy her time.

Carter Jensen likes his quiet, uneventful life in Monroe Falls. Widowed for seven years now, he's content to stow away in his upstairs office, working with his antique maps and avoiding as many people as he can. But when the attractive travel writer Sky Emerson shows up unannounced to write an article on his business, his solitude is threatened. He's determined to get rid of this city girl as quickly as possible. Though the more time he spends with her, the more surprises she seems to have in store for him.

Will Carter reel her in? Or will his fear of letting down the ones he loves cause Sky to be the one who got away?

ABOUT THE AUTHORS

Meet the authors of the Monroe Falls Romance Novellas:
   Jules Dixon
   Fuzzy sock collector, martini connoisseur, and dandelion enthusiast, author Jules Dixon writes contemporary and LGBT romance, weaving sizzle and humor into both short and long stories. Find a rainbow of happily ever afters at www.julesdixon.com.
   You can join Jules here:
   Facebook:
   http://www.facebook.com/JulesDixonAuthor
   Twitter:
   https://twitter.com/JulesofTripleR
   Pinterest:
   https://www.pinterest.com/JDixonAuthor
   Book & Main:
   https://bookandmainbites.com/JulesDixonAuthor
   Instagram:
   https://www.instagram.com/julesdixonauthor/
   Other titles by Jules Dixon:
   Triple R Series—
   Run to Love: Triple R 1

Rest, My Love: Triple R 2
Ride With Love: Triple R 3
Road to Love: Triple R 4
Ready to Love: Triple R 5
Ribbons of Love: Triple R 6
Rescued by Love: Triple R 7
Cherry County Cowboys Series—
Spurs: Cherry County Cowboys 1
Chaps: Cherry County Cowboys 2
Whips: Cherry County Cowboys 3
Other Anthologies with Jules' stories—
Owned by the Alpha: Manlove Edition
Holiday Hotties Short Stories Collection—
Winter Wishes
Snowflake Smiles
Candy Cane Cupid
Mistletoe Mine
Jingle Bell Joy
Champagne Cheers
Frozen Faith

Nikki Hyson

Nikki Hyson started writing at the age of 8 when her library ran out of horse stories. Since then she's dabbled in nearly every genre, but leans towards speculative fiction. She loves autumn walks with her dogs, cooking for friends, and NaNoWriMo. She has faith in nights.

You can join Nikki here:

Facebook:

https://www.facebook.com/NikkiHysonWrites/

Twitter:

https://twitter.com/NikkiHyson

Other stories from Nikki coming soon, including a sweet romance series!

Kristin Lee

Known for using whimsy at will, binging on British television, and attempting to always be the most sarcastic person in the room, author Kristin Lee enjoys creating contemporary romance stories with heart, guts, and humor in dramatic situations...imagine that. And there's that sarcasm. New romantic comedy coming fall 2018!

You can join Kristin here:

Instagram:

https://www.instagram.com/kristinleeauthor/

Facebook:

https://www.facebook.com/kristinleeauthor

Cynthia Morton

Cynthia Morton enjoys writing contemporary, paranormal, and young adult romance. She is a complete romantic at heart who enjoys British television and a good book. With her love of traveling and history, she plans to backpack the British Isles one day.

You can join Cynthia here:

Facebook:

https://www.facebook.com/WriterCynthiaMorton/

Instagram:

https://www.instagram.com/writer.cynthiamorton/

Wynter S.K.

Wynter S.K. hails from Lincoln, Neb., and currently resides in Omaha with her husband and three furkids—Teddy, the Pushy Pomeranian, Gatsby, the new Pushy Pomeranian, and Lucky, the Contemptuous Cat (or, just Cat, because...cats). She's a graduate of UNL (GO BIG RED!) and recently obtained her MFA in Creative Writing from Creighton (GO JAYS!). Her razor-sharp romances will require you to strap yourself in, because they'll take you for one hell of a ride! Coming Soon, Santarossa Red!

You can join Wynter here:
Facebook:
https://www.facebook.com/WynterSK/
Twitter:
https://twitter.com/Wynter_SK
Instagram:
https://www.instagram.com/wynter_sk/
Other titles by Wynter:
Pas de Deux
Wynter also writes as Meredith Allison.

Jacqueline Winters-

Jacqueline Winters has been writing since she was nine when she'd sneak stacks of paper from her grandma's closet and fill them with adventure. She grew up in Small-Town Nebraska, and spent a decade living in beautiful Alaska. She writes contemporary romances, some set in small Nebraskan towns, and a series coming soon set in charming Alaskan locations.

She's a sucker for happily ever afters, has a sweet tooth that can be sated with cupcakes, and firmly believes sangria was possibly the best invention ever. On a relaxing evening, you can find her at her computer writing her next novel with her dog poking his adorable head out from beneath the desk. Coming Soon from Jacqueline—*Cowboys and Starlight*, a heart-warming love story.

You can join Jacqueline here:
Facebook:
https://www.facebook.com/JacquelineWintersRomance/
Twitter:
https://twitter.com/jwintersak
Other titles by Jacqueline:
Sweetly Scandalous (A Willow Creek Novel Book 1)
Secretly Scandalous (A Willow Creek Novel Book 2)
Simply Scandalous (A Willow Creek Novel Book 3)

ACKNOWLEDGMENTS

Robert-your arms inspired this story. I love being in them and having you in mine. May our love see another 25+ years. <3 Julie

Nanette-MODERN <3 4EVER. I cherish that we've become more than mentor and newbie. You are my friend. I know it's scary, sorry. Thank you for all your advice and camaraderie while I trudge onward.

Michelle Morgan-your edits and insights on all my past stories are what made this one what it is. Thank you for everything. Hugs.

Meredith-thank you for polishing the Epilogue. I swear Dragon likes you better than he does me.

The ladies of my critique group-I dedicated this to you, but that doesn't cover all of the gratitude I have to you. It's a list that's never ending. Can't wait to see what the next year has in store for everyone. Love you all.